Ruby's Dream

THE STORY OF

Ronan Matthew

ISS Publishing

Brooklyn, New York

1

Ronan Matthew
11322 Castor Street
Las Vegas, Nevada 89183

Ruby's Dream: The Story of a Boy's Life - by Ronan Matthew
ISBN 978-1-7367028-0-2

Contents

Ruby's Dream is the story of a young Caribbean boy's life as he struggles to fulfill his own dream to overcome the difficult circumstances of his existence. He is the youngest of his mother's six children. Unfortunately, he experienced the death of his mother when he was only six years old. He met his abusive father sometime when he was around the age of ten. The abusive behavior of his alcoholic father caused the six children to be homeless before he became a teenager. Times were tough living in the colonial Caribbean. Because of the tough circumstance of day-to-day life, he sought refuge in his friends who did not always accept him because of his physical appearance. He grew up in a black world with white skin. His white skin was on account of the exploitation of black women by his European grandfather, who never acknowledged his mother. Despite the odds, he persevered and achieved a modicum of success.

Ruby's Dream tells the story of Terrence Antonio, a boy who refused to be cast aside by society because he believed that he had the ability to make a better life for himself.

◊◊

Chapter 1

Terrence had felt extremely confident, and optimistic on this Monday morning as he walked in an easterly direction on 125th Street. He was on his way to the subway station at 125th Street and Lexington Avenue, there he would take the train to 42nd Street at Grand Central Station.

This was the first time that he was going out to find a job. He was_confident that he would be successful in this endeavor. He had done the necessary research and he thought that finding a job that he wanted would not have been difficult. There was no reason to expect or contemplate failure in his search for employment. His confidence and optimism came from the fact that he had purchased the New York Times the previous day and had diligently explored the want-ads. He had come upon an advertised position to work for the airlines and decided to apply for it.

Everything on East 125th Street was the same as he had seen it for the past two months that he had been living in New York City in an area called Harlem. It was not yet eight o'clock on this Monday morning, however, drug addicts and winos were already standing on the steps and doorways of buildings along the street. Some had spent the entire night standing out on the street or sleeping in the hallways of buildings. He had learned that this was a normal occurrence during the summer months when it was extremely hot and humid. It was now the middle of August 1970.

To get to Lexington Avenue, from Madison Avenue where he lived, he had to first pass Park Avenue. A number of winos and drug addicts were standing at the exit of the Penn Central Railway station at 125th Street and Park Avenue. As he walked by, one of them asked him for a quarter and said it was to buy a cup of coffee. He ignored the beggar and continued on his way to the subway station. He had already learned that it was not wise to give money to beggars on the street, especially those that were drug addicts and winos. The money was unlikely to be used for coffee but instead for drugs or cheap wine. He had noticed, as he passed by, that the Penn Central policemen also stood in close proximity to the drug addicts and winos. The Penn Central policemen were different to the other policemen of the New York City Police Department who patrolled the streets by car and by foot. The Penn Central policemen only patrolled the railway cars and the railway stations. He wondered why the policemen did not order the beggars to disperse.

Park Avenue and 125th Street was a stop on the Penn Central Railroad. This railway line was not a part of the New York City subway system. It was a railway line which left Grand Central Station and took passengers north to the affluent upstate suburbs of New York such as Mamaroneck, Scarsdale and the City of New Haven in Connecticut. Not many passengers boarded or disembarked at this stop. It appeared that the policemen were assigned here to ensure the protection of the few passengers as they entered and left the station. The station generally was not very busy. The policemen appeared not to have much to do, except to ensure that the passengers were not bothered by the winos and heroin addicts who loitered around the station. The policemen kept a close eye on these vagrants as much as possible and tried to prevent them from harassing the passengers.

On the next block, he was accosted once again, this time by a man asking for spare change. This man was in terrible shape. He was in a trancelike state and could not keep his eyes open. This beggar's partially extended arm was swollen to more than twice its normal size and filled with scabrous sores. These scabrous sores were evidence of heroin use, the result of years of using a hypodermic needle to inject heroin directly into the veins of his arm.

In the past, he had wondered what had caused persons to resort to using heroin, when the evidence of its devastating effects was all around them. Why would someone voluntarily use this drug, when its debilitating effects were always evident? It was difficult for him to understand. On this day, instead of feeling pity for the heroin addicts, he tried his best to concentrate on the job that he would be applying for.

He had been told by more than one of his American teachers who had come to Santa Maria as religious brothers, that the people in the ghettos of America were responsible for their situation. Harlem in 1970 was considered a ghetto. The inhabitants of the ghettos were said to have no ambition, all they wanted was fun for the moment. They took drugs and excessively drank alcohol, as a result they wasted their lives away. To him, this explanation had been too simplistic, and he often thought that there was a deeper meaning to this abandonment of hope that was evident in the eyes of the heroin addicts and the winos on East 125th Street. Now, he was focused on finding employment after living in Harlem for a couple of months. He wanted to be employed so that he could start the process of building a successful life.

He felt assured that he was appropriately dressed. He was wearing his only suit, a shiny black double-breasted sharkskin which had been bought by his sister for him to wear to the funeral of his father, a father that he never really knew, who had died two weeks earlier.

He wanted it to be his day, the day that would start him off on a path to a new life. He would present himself to the employment agency and he would be hired. This was the feeling of optimism that he had left home with on this Monday morning.

He reached Lexington Avenue, turned left and headed down into the subway. At the token booth, he encountered a long line. As it was a Monday morning, many subway riders were purchasing their supply of tokens for the entire week. The fact that he encountered a long line at the token booth and that hundreds of other persons who had previously purchased their tokens were rushing into the station to take the train downtown to work, meant, of course, that the people of Harlem were not all slackers and idlers. In fact, they had jobs which they were rushing to.

On the lower part of the station, which was the downtown platform, there were hundreds of people waiting to get on the train. This was a transfer point for persons wishing to use the express train to get to their jobs in a shorter period of time. The number four express seemed to be more favorable to the local number six which stopped at all the stations on its way to Grand Central Station. The express number four stopped only two times before reaching Grand Central Station, his destination.

As the express train pulled into the 125th Street station, the crowd made a great surge forward towards the doors before the train came to a complete stop. Because the passengers had carried out this ritual hundreds of times before, they knew exactly where the doors would line up to the platform after the train stopped. When the doors opened, the crowd on the platform continued their surge forward without waiting for the incoming passengers who wished to disembark. The disembarking passengers at 125th Street had to make a great effort to squeeze their way past the surging crowd getting on the train. He was amazed by this circumstance and became an on-looker. He did not join the crowd in the great rush but stood off to the side waiting for the rush to subside. As a result of his hesitation, the doors started to close before he boarded the train and as he tried to enter, the doors closed in his face. To his dismay, he had missed the train. The train left the station without him. He felt an awkwardness and promised to correct the mistake which he had just made. In a few minutes, another train entered the station and this time he was more aggressive in getting on and was barely successful. He managed to squeeze himself through the doors, as they closed, he was caught in the middle and the doors retracted. The retraction allowed him time to enter, because it gave him a few extra seconds.

Once on board the train, there were no seats available. The train was packed with people and he wondered if it was better to sit or stand on a crowded train as it sped through the tunnel. The train was overcrowded to the extent that it was virtually impossible to move or turn in any direction without causing discomfort to himself or others who were next to him. He later found out that this overcrowding was customary on any workday because the number four express originated in an area of the North Bronx called Woodlawn, before making its first stop in Manhattan at 125th Street and Lexington Avenue. The train had already taken on the passengers from the Bronx, on their way to their jobs in mid and lower Manhattan and the financial district of Wall Street. It was also full of passengers who had taken the number six local train from an area in the Bronx called Pelham to 125th Street and then transferred to the express to continue their journey to the eastside of Manhattan. The official name of the express number four train was the Woodlawn Express. The number six train was officially the Pelham Local.

He had a feeling of discomfort as he tried to settle himself for the journey to Grand Central Station. He was not accustomed to situations like this where he had to surrender his territorial space to persons whom he did not know. There were no passenger trains on Santa Maria, the small Caribbean island from which he had emigrated only two months before. The only trains he had seen before were the locomotive trains which were used to take the sugar cane crop from the estates to the sugar factory to be processed into sugar before being shipped to the United Kingdom. The sole sugar factory was located in an area called Gunthorpes which was geographically almost the center of the island. The sugar estates in Santa Maria were owned by the British and they built these locomotive trains. They were built during the time that Santa Maria was a British colony, and the sugar industry was a great contributing factor to the wealth of the United Kingdom. In 1967, Santa Maria became an Associated State of the United Kingdom. This status remained in place until 1981 when the island became a fully independent nation. These trains were no longer in use because it was difficult to get replacement parts to keep them well maintained and functional. In the middle sixties, the planters who owned the sugar industry opted to transport the sugar crop from the estates to the sugar factory by tractors. By this time 'King Sugar' as the industry was euphemistically called, was dying out. The local leadership of the island had started the move away from agriculture to tourism as the main driver of the economy.

In Santa Maria, there were passenger busses. Terrence seldom ever rode on a bus because he had lived in the city and public transportation was not needed to get from one place to the next in the city. The most common method of getting from one place to the next was by walking. Virtually every place he needed to go was in walking distance from the house where he lived.

It appeared that the other passengers were detached from the situation of being on the overcrowded train. There was no eye contact with other passengers. He noticed that if he looked directly at someone and their eyes met, that person would almost immediately look away. Some passengers passed the time by reading the newspaper. The popular newspapers for the passengers on the train were the New York Daily News and the New York Post. The business types who mostly entered at 86th Street and 59th Street, read the Wall Street Journal and the New York Times. Though unaccustomed to this type of circumstance, where everyone seemed detached from the other, he tried to maintain his high level of expectation and enthusiasm regarding the position he had seen in the New York Times. This newspaper was known for having the most comprehensive classified section in its Sunday Edition. There were thousands of jobs listed each Sunday and he imagined that they were not difficult to get. It was just a matter of buying the newspaper and finding an advertisement for the job he wanted and then present himself to the agency which advertised the job or in some cases, the application could be made directly to the company. In general, most of the available jobs advertised required the applicant to go through an agency. In some cases, the advertisement put out by the agency had a fine print that indicated that there was a fee which was the responsibility of the applicant, if he was successful in securing a position. Other times, to a lesser extent, there was an indication that the fee would be paid by the employer. He did not recall whether or not the advertisement which caught his interest and for which he was about to apply, indicated on whose shoulders the fee would rest. Not all of the want-ads indicated that there would be a fee.

As the train moved away from 125th Street, it picked up speed through the tunnel. He stood there, making sure that he kept his balance at the same time wondering if he too would acquire the air of detachment that he noticed on the other passengers. After all, he figured that he too would be taking the subway on a daily basis after he was able to get this position which he sought. He deduced that the aloof coldness and detachment of passengers on a New York City subway was not acquired after one or two experiences of rush hour.

The subway ride to Grand Central Station lasted less than fifteen minutes with two quick stops, the first at 86th Street and the second at 59th Street. The arrival of the train at Grand Central Station was much like its arrival at 125th Street. Most of the passengers disembarked in the same way they had entered the train at 125th Street. They all pushed to get off the train in a mad frenzy. He was one of the last to exit and was lucky not to have the doors close before he could get off. Getting on and off packed subway trains was a skill that he would have to develop if he was going to use them on a daily basis to get to work and back. Even though all the other passengers rushed off the train at this stop, the rush appeared to be learned, a subconscious skill developed from doing a task over and over.

His destination was the iconic art deco Chrysler Building located in the vicinity of Lexington Avenue and 42nd Street. The Action Airline Employment Agency was located on the fifty-fifth floor. After exiting the subway at Grand Central Station at 42nd Street, he made a left and headed to Lexington Avenue. As a newcomer to New York City, he was fascinated by the grandeur of Grand Central Station but decided that he would look around the station on his return. He felt that he could hold his fascination for later in the day when he returned from securing the position which he sought and for which he had made this journey to the east side of mid-town Manhattan.

He had seen the Chrysler Building before on a previous trip to Manhattan. It was very tall and rivaled the Empire State Building located on 34th Street and 6th Avenue, also called Avenue of the Americas. He assumed that the building had some connection to the Chrysler car company but was not sure. He entered the building and looked for the Action Airline Employment Agency in the building directory. Next to the directory was a bank of elevators and above each of the six elevators, was demarcated the floors that the individual elevators serviced. He entered the elevator that indicated that it would take him to the fifty-fifth floor and pushed the button and was on his way. The thought of going on an elevator to the fifty-fifth floor of a building was quite intimidating to someone who had lived all of his life on an island which, at the time, had an unwritten rule that no building could be 'taller than a coconut tree'. The Chrysler Building was indeed many times the height of a coconut tree.

It was said that one of the former leaders of the island had said that no building should be taller than a coconut tree and the saying became a rule which was practiced from then on. In all likelihood it was not a rule at all, it was something that was said, and it became a part of the local folklore. The saying was abandoned and set aside with the development of tourism as the main driver of the economy. Tourism necessitated the building of large hotels. Many of the hotels disregarded the folklore that no building could be taller than a coconut tree and had three and four floors which were indeed taller than coconut trees.

Another saying which became a part of the local folklore and even used consistently in tourist promotions to market the island was that 'Santa Maria had 365 beaches', one for every day of the year. Santa Maria indeed has many beaches which are unimaginably beautiful, but it was never determined that there were actually 365. Many of the beaches on the island could not be reached by car because there were no roads which led to them, consequently, they could only be accessed by sea. Many persons have circumnavigated the island with the purpose of counting all the beaches and none of them ever got close to counting 365.

Apparently, the idea of using the slogan of 365 beaches, one for every day of the year came about after the nearby island of Dominica used a slogan to promote their tourism. That slogan was 'the island with 365 rivers. Hence, if rivers were abundant in Dominica and they used the slogan '365 rivers' to promote their island and beaches were abundant in Santa Maria then Santa Maria could also use the slogan '365 beaches' as a tourism promotion.

He exited the elevator on the fifty-fifth floor and set about to find the office that he was looking for. After finding the office, he did not enter, but decided that he should use the restroom first to calm himself. He was a bit nervous because he had never been on a formal job interview before, and he wanted to relieve his nervousness. Before leaving the restroom, he looked into the mirror to reassure himself that he had not become disheveled from the overcrowded subway ride. After a few pats to his budding Afro haircut, which he started to grow since his arrival in New York, he walked briskly out of the restroom, down the hallway and opened the door of the Action Airline Employment Agency.

As he entered, he noticed a reception desk but there was no one sitting there. He looked around and saw two other persons sitting in the office. He assumed that they were also applicants because they were seated in a waiting area. One was male and the other female. If they were competitors for the position that he sought, he reasoned that he might have a better chance than they did because they were not appropriately dressed for a job interview. The male had not bothered to wear a suit. He was casually dressed in slacks and a shirt. The female was also dressed in slacks and was wearing a simple blouse with buttons on the front. There was a handbag on the seat next to her, so he made the assumption that it was hers. Next to the handbag on the same seat was a folded copy of the Sunday Edition of the New York Times. The classified section was visible when he did a cursory glance where they were sitting. Most likely, she too had seen the job vacancy printed in the newspaper and had come for the same reason that brought him here to the fifty-fifth floor of the Chrysler Building to find employment in the airline industry.

After standing at the reception desk for about thirty seconds, a young lady who was no more than twenty-two years old came from an inner office to greet him.

"Good morning, may I help you?" she asked.

"Good morning," he replied. "I am here to apply for the airline trainee position which I saw advertised in the classified section of yesterday's New York Times."

"Please sit in this chair," she said pointing to the chair next to the reception desk. "I have to ask you a few questions."

He looked to see if she was wearing a name tag, he wanted to address her by name. She was not wearing a name tag, so he responded by simply saying thank you and sat in the chair next to the desk as she had instructed him to do. She sat in the chair behind the desk and took out an application form from the top drawer. She did not hand it to him, instead, she proceeded to ask him questions and wrote the answers on the form herself.

"What is your name?" she asked.

"My name is Terrence Antonio," he replied.

"How old are you?" was the next question.

"I am eighteen years old," was his reply.

He answered her questions in a polite manner wondering why she simply did not hand him the application form so that he could fill it out himself. He wondered if she thought that he was not intelligent enough to answer the questions and fill out the form himself or was she just being kind? She continued with the questioning.

"Did you graduate from high school?" he was asked.

"Yes, I did," he responded with enthusiasm.

"When did you graduate?" she asked.

"I graduated from high school in June of this year," he responded again with enthusiasm.

"What is the name of your high school?" she continued.

"I attended St. Mary's High School," he responded and also added, "It might be easier if I filled out the form so that you do not have to fill the form as I give the answers."
This seemed like a reasonable thing to say but his statement regarding filling out the form himself was ignored.

"Is this a Catholic school?" she asked.

"Yes, it is a Catholic high school," he said.

"Where is this school located?" she asked.

"My high school is located on Santa Maria island in the West Indies."

"So you are from the West Indies, I heard your accent. I suppose that you are not an American citizen, this agency gives preference to American citizens." This statement was said with firmness.

Her last statement took him by surprise. However, he was not alarmed, she had heard his distinct accent and immediately came to the conclusion that he was not an American citizen.

"I am not an American citizen as yet, I have my permanent residency, I have my green card which entitles me to work in the

United States," he responded confidently. He had only just received his treasured green card in the mail.

He arrived at Kennedy Airport in New York on June 18th, 1970. He had his chemistry final exam slated on June 18th, but he had to forego taking this exam because his immigration papers stated that they would be null and void if he arrived in the United States after this date. He was not good in science and felt that he might not have passed this exam even if he had the time to take it but as it worked out, he had to leave on that day before taking it. Upon seeing the examination schedule and knowing that he was unable to take it due to the time conflicts, he did not study for chemistry. He figured that there was no point in studying for an examination which he would not be present to take. He focused his attention on his other subjects for which he would be present. When he presented his documents to the immigration officer upon his arrival at Kennedy Airport the officer commented,

"You just barely made it."

He did not respond to the comment of the immigration officer and the immigration officer asked him why he had not arrived sooner. He then told the immigration officer that he had to take his final exams for his graduation from high school before he left. He did not tell him that he missed out on taking his chemistry final and that he did not bother to study for it.

He had received his permanent residency visa in February of that year after traveling to Barbados with his sister to the American Embassy for the Eastern Caribbean. Their arrival in Barbados was at 8:30 pm aboard BWIA, which was the national airline of Trinidad and Tobago. Though it was the national airline for Trinidad and Tobago, the official name was British West Indies International Airlines. Locals in the Caribbean called it Bee Wee and others called the airline less complimentary names such as Better Walk If Able, suggesting that the airline was not dependable. After going through immigration and customs in Barbados, he and his sister caught a taxi to the Crystal Crest Guest House located in St. Michael, not very far from the U.S. Embassy in the capital, Bridgetown. The taxi driver appeared to be a kind man who said that he would get them safely and quickly to the guesthouse. He was true to his word and they arrived safely in a very short period of time. At the time, there was no U.S. Embassy in Santa Maria, the closest U.S. embassy was in Barbados and persons from the other islands in the Eastern Caribbean who needed visas to travel to the United States had to expend a significant amount of money to travel to Barbados to be interviewed by the U.S. Embassy staff before the visa was issued.

Barbados was approximately sixty square miles larger than Santa Maria but had three times the population. It was more developed and had a reputation for orderliness which was in contrast to that of Santa Maria. This island had a literacy rate of 98%. This literacy rate exceeded that of the other islands of the Caribbean, and it was something in which the people of Barbados took great pride. They also took pride in their island being called "Little England". It was said that it was because of the orderliness of the island that this moniker was given. During the colonial period, it was one of the major sugar-producing islands. It was said that many of the islands had absentee plantation owners but in Barbados, many of the owners took up residence there.

What endeared Terrence to this island was that it was the birthplace and home of his cricket idol, Garry Sobers. On the short journey to the guesthouse, he asked the driver many questions about this cricketer who, at the time, was the best cricketer in the world. Garry Sobers could bat, he could bowl in three different styles and he was a brilliant fielder. In addition to those obvious talents, Garry Sobers held the world record for scoring the highest individual score in a test match and he accomplished this gargantuan feat when he was only twenty-one years old. A former cricket captain of England, Ted Dexter, described him thus,

"In cricket, there are good players, there are very good players, there are excellent players, there are superb players and there are magnificent players, well Garry Sobers stands alone, he was the most superb of the magnificent."

He had met his cricket idol two years before at a cricket match in Santa Maria. He was almost in tears when his idol did not do well in the first innings of the match. Garry Sobers, to his dismay, was bowled behind his back by a local cricketer called Dougla. Dougla was not his given name at birth. The name Dougla was a term used to describe a person of Indian and African ancestry. This was particularly common in Trinidad and Guyana, two countries which had high percentages of persons with Indian and African ancestries.

Sobers' many fans were very disappointed and, of course, others rejoiced in the success of the local player. The adulation given to the local player was short lived. In the second innings, as soon as Sobers came out to bat, the crowd began to chant the name of the local player shouting at the top of their lungs, "We want Dougla." They wanted Dougla and they got him. The captain of the local team granted the wish of the spectators and summoned Dougla to bowl to the great Garry Sobers. No sooner than he was put on to bowl his leg spinners, Garry Sobers launched into him and hit him for fours and sixes to all corners of the cricket field. The particular shot that Terrence remembered most was a flick for six. Garry Sobers was batting at the southern end of the field or what was then called the Factory Road End. Dougla was bowling from the Pavilion End.

He ran in to bowl and tossed up the ball on the leg side expecting it to turn into the left-handed Garry Sobers. He calmly put his right foot forward and with the lighting speed movement of his wrists, flicked the ball for six. It was a scintillating shot that mesmerized not only the crowd but also the players on the field. That was the end of Dougla's bowling spell. No other bowler was a match for the great Garry Sobers and he retired and allowed others to bat.

Terrence had gone to the match with a picture of his hero in his pocket hoping to get it autographed by him. On the first day, he was too despondent to try to meet him after he was out for a low score. On the second day, things were different. Sobers conquered all the bowlers and Terrence was happy. He decided that he would meet him and get his picture signed. He had gotten this picture from his pen-pal who lived in Barbados. In all of his letters to his pen-pal, he spoke about his admiration for Garry Sobers. She eventually sent him a picture of a smiling Garry Sobers in his cricketing whites, with a Banks beer, the national beer of Barbados, in his hands. He treasured this picture and he wanted to get it signed by the man himself. It was at the end of play for the day, and he decided to make his move. Cricket matches can last up to five days. He could have waited until the players came out of their dressing room and walked to their busses to leave the stadium, but he felt that he would have a better chance of approaching him directly if he sneaked into the dressing room and presented the photograph to him for his autograph.

When the policeman who was guarding the back entrance to the players pavilion looked away, Terrence jumped over the fence and walked up the steps as if he belonged there. He knew one of the players on the local team and he told him what he wanted to do. Fortunately for him, the local player did not call the policeman, but he also did not help him any further. To get inside the locker room was another task that he had to figure out, he could not go through the door because there was another policeman standing there and, of course, he did not have a badge which gave him permission to enter. The locker room had a window that was half open. He had reached this far and was not about to turn back before getting the desired autograph. He looked through the window and saw Garry Sobers sitting with his teammates. Now was his chance, he quickly climbed through the window, which was half open before he could be noticed, and in a flash, he presented the photograph to his idol and asked him to sign it. Garry Sobers looked at the picture and asked,

"Where did you get this?"
Garry Sobers was actually speaking to him and for a moment he was too star struck to answer. A second or two passed before he got back his composure and said,

"I have a pen-pal in Barbados who sent it to me."

Garry Sobers smiled and signed the picture and gave it back to him and shook his hand. He turned and climbed back through the half open window that he came in. This time as he exited, he did not climb over the fence as he had come in, he simply walked down the steps and through the gate where the policeman was still standing guard to prevent others like him from entering.

Outside, he showed the signed autographed picture to his friends who looked at it with a bit of jealousy. Terrence studied the signature and decided that he would copy the way Sobers made the G of his first name. From then on, all of his capital Gs were signed the way that Sobers did.

In the car to the Crystal Crest Guest House, he asked the taxi driver if he would be willing to take him to show him where Garry Sobers lived. He was hoping that if he was taken there, maybe he would be lucky enough to get a glimpse of Garry

Sobers. He knew that it was unlikely for him to see his idol but, in reality, he just wanted to see where he lived.

The taxi driver turned down his request and said that he knew where he lived but that Sobers was away in England. He was disappointed but he did not insist, he simply asked the taxi driver if he could return to the guest house to take them to the U.S. Embassy for their 9:00am appointment the next morning and the taxi driver agreed. The taxi driver arrived at 8:30am the following morning and they arrived at the embassy in time for their appointment.

The appointment at the U.S. Embassy was completed without a hitch. All of their papers were in order and the consular officer, congratulated them on qualifying as permanent residents of the United States.

His sister who was older than he was, left for the United States shortly after returning to Santa Maria. He, on the other hand, stayed back to complete most of his final exams which were scheduled before the June 18th, 1970 deadline for him to migrate to the United States. The high school final exam dates could not have been changed because they were stipulated by Cambridge University in England. The exams were composed in England and sent to the English 'colonies' and 'former colonies' in the Caribbean. After the exams were completed, they were shipped back to England to be graded. The results were sent back to the schools in the middle of August of each year. Some students who did not do well on these exams which could determine their entire future opted to return to school to repeat their senior year. This would allow them the opportunity to take the exams for the second time. If successful, their chances of securing positions in the job market would be greatly improved.

After their return to the guest house from the embassy, he called a friend who was attending the University of the West Indies in Barbados. His friend had graduated from St. Mary's High School two years before and had managed to be accepted to study at this university which was considered to be quite prestigious. He had seen other students from his island who had returned to Santa Maria after graduation from the University of the West Indies and everything about them was different. They were highly respected in society and they also acted with an air of superiority. It was as if they knew that they were expected to act this way. They seemed to have lost all sense of humility. They were now part of the intellectual elite of Santa Maria. Fortunately, for he and his sister, his friend had not yet completed his university studies and he had not yet acquired this air of superiority and intellectual elitism.

At the time, Santa Maria, did not have daily newspapers. The two newspapers were intermittent and were not dependable to bring up to date news. As a result, because of the close proximity to Santa Maria, a newspaper called the Barbados Advocate was sent by plane to Santa Maria every day with the exception of Sunday. This newspaper was popular, and it was widely read in Santa Maria. The sports section was of particular interest to Terrence because he could get all the new information about his beloved West Indies cricket team. Most of the players on the team, at the time, were from Barbados and the news about the team was quite up to date.

The Barbados Advocate also had an entertainment section. Several times, he had read stories and had seen pictures of a new discotheque that had opened in Barbados. It appeared from the articles written about it that this discotheque was becoming very popular on the island. He asked his friend who was attending the university, if he could take them to this new discotheque called the Cats Whiskers. His friend was surprised because he had never been there, but he agreed to take them that night.

The discotheque was very upscale. It was in an upstairs building in the heart of the capital. The patrons were all fashionably dressed. There was a mix of locals and foreigners. While there, he met one of the players on the West Indies cricket team. Charlie Griffith, one of the fearsome bowlers who made up the duo of Hall and Griffith, walked in with friends. It seemed like it would have been impolite to ask for his autograph under those circumstances so instead he nodded when he walked by and told him that he was a fan. He had seen Charlie Griffith bowl in person before while the West Indies cricket team had made a stopover in Santa Maria after a tour of England. The Santa Maria cricket team was practicing at the local cricket field and because the West Indies team was on a layover, some of the team members went over to the field. The best batsman for Santa Maria was taking batting practice. The ball was given to Charlie Griffith to bowl at this batsman from Santa Maria. Maybe it was nervousness, but the first couple of balls bowled by Charlie Griffith, had the batsman in all kinds of difficulty. He was running away from the ball instead of facing it head on. The Santa Marian spectators that were witnessing the practice hoped that the local player would have done well, and this might have given him a chance to show his ability and more importantly to play for the West Indies. This was an opportunity for him to shine but things did not go well for the local player, running from the ball was not a good way to make a positive impression. Charlie Griffith saw that he was afraid of the ball or maybe he was afraid of the man, Charlie Griffith, and decided to bowl much more slowly. The local player's reputation was tarnished, and he receded into oblivion as a cricketer. He never got the chance to play for the West Indies. He was always remembered as the batsman who ran away from the bowling of Charlie Griffith because of fear.

The morning after their night out at the Cats Whiskers discotheque, he and his sister flew back to Santa Maria with their permanent residency visas which entitled them to live and work permanently in the United States.

Terrence reached into his pocket for his wallet and took out his green card and showed it to the interviewer. She perused it carefully as if she believed that there was a possibility that it could have been a fake document. In reality, it looked very new because it was new. She then asked,

"When did you get this?"

"I received it in the mail on Friday," he responded.

He had indeed received it in the mail on the previous Friday, six weeks after he had been told that he would. The delay in receiving his green card was caused by an error on the part of the immigration officer who processed his visa upon his arrival at Kennedy Airport on June 18[th,] 1970. The immigration officer told him that he would receive his green card in two weeks from the immigration office located in lower Manhattan. The immigration officer had made the mistake of returning all the documents to him. Unaware that the immigration officer had made a mistake by returning all his documents to him, Terrence took home the documents in the brown manila envelope and kept it in his suitcase. After two weeks had passed and he did not receive the green card in the mail, he looked up the address of the immigration office and journeyed there on his own to find out what was causing the delay. He waited on a line for three hours to finally get the opportunity to talk to one of their employees at the counter. He was then told to be patient and that it would come in the mail shortly. The employee did not ask for his name or check any records, he just told him to be patient. Terrence did not get the opportunity to present the documents in the manila envelope even though he had taken them with him. He was still unaware that a mistake had been made. If he was aware, he might have tried to be more forceful in presenting the documents which he had in his possession.

After another two weeks went by and he still had not received his green card, he made another journey to the immigration office. He again carried the brown manila envelope with his documents inside. After another three-hour wait, he was at the head of the line and was able to speak with the employee stationed there to answer questions at the counter. This time, before asking the question, he pulled out the documents from the manila envelope and told the employee that he had been waiting for a month before receiving his green card in the mail. To his surprise the employee said,

"Why do you have this?" pointing to the documents, "You are not supposed to have this. You are never going to get your green card if you have this in your possession. Why didn't they take it from you at the airport when you arrived?"

He was dumb struck and did not know what to say. He simply managed,

"I don't know."

The employee took the documents from him and said,

"You will get it in the mail in two weeks."

Thus, the mystery of the missing green card was solved. The green card arrived in two weeks. He finished his application, but he was not successful in finding a job with the Action Airline Employment Agency. After finding out that he was not an American citizen, the discussion went downhill. She recommended that he should consider accepting a position as a messenger. He pointed out that he was interested in the position that he had seen advertised in the New York Times the previous day. He went on to say that he was not interested in being a messenger, he wanted to apply to the airlines.

He imagined that his West Indian accent might have played a role, but he was not sure, however, it was a thought that would always cross his mind in the future when he sought employment. He also knew that he was proud of his West Indian accent and he did not plan to change it. He would never put on an American accent just to fit in. His grandmother, Catherine Thomas or Aunt Kitty, as she was called by all of her relatives, had lived in the United States for almost fifty years and she still spoke very much like a Santa Marian. She was a proud woman who moved to New York City in 1925 to seek out a better life for herself and her two children.

His grandmother had been called Aunt Kitty by everyone who knew her including her own two daughters, her grandchildren, her sisters and other members of her extended family. Terrence wondered why everyone referred to her as Aunt Kitty when he knew that she was not their aunt. At the time of his mother's death, he was only six years old, and he had never met his grandmother, but he remembered that his mother referred to this mythical figure as Aunt Kitty. Even though she lived in the United States and was not around them, she was spoken of with reverence. She was spoken of in this manner because she was a source of support to the family. She was away when he was born in August of 1952 and she did not return to Santa Maria to attend the funeral of her daughter, his mother, in August of 1959. At the time, he did not know what she did for a living in the United States. He only knew that she lived there and to the people of Santa Maria, everyone who lived there was rich.

His quest to work for an airline came to an end that Monday morning. The interviewer was insistent that he should consider being a messenger and he was insistent that he was not interested in that line of work.

He left the office feeling that he had not been treated fairly. He was confused. He did not feel as if he had done anything wrong. He went into that office with his West Indian pride and he left with it intact. He reasoned that the problem was not his, the problem was hers. He felt that he was qualified for the position because the want-ad stated that the only qualification was that the applicant must have graduated from high school and he was a high school graduate. He also knew that five of his friends who recently graduated from high school in Santa Maria had gained employment with the airlines. He felt that he was just as qualified as they were.

He took the elevator back down to the ground floor and exited the building. Instead of heading over to Grand Central Station, he decided that he would explore 42nd Street. His planned exploration of Grand Central Station was put off for another time. He walked easterly until he got to the East River. From here, he could see the Borough of Queens, but what was more fascinating was that he could see the buildings of the United Nations. He walked north on 1st Avenue and was taken aback when he saw an apartment building that was actually built over the Eastside Highway. The cars on the highway appeared to go through the building. He was already impressed with the architecture of New York City. He had heard the term 'concrete jungle' used to describe cities, but he did not conceptualize the meaning until he saw the tall buildings which appeared to kiss the sky. He had never seen a jungle because there were no jungles in Santa Maria. On the south side of the island was an area called the rain forest, but it was not really a forest. It was called that simply because the entire island was dry and had very little rainfall, and in this area, it rained marginally more than the other parts of the island. To get to this area called the rain forest you had to drive on a road called Fig Tree Drive. It is ironic that this road is called Fig Tree Drive because figs do not grow in Santa Maria. In Santa Maria, bananas are called figs and many bananas are grown on this side of the island, hence the name Fig Tree Drive. Travelers on this road can see the banana fields on both sides of the road.

He walked back to 42nd Street and walked west to Times Square. He had previously heard of Times Square and had seen it on television and remembered it as the place where thousands of people from all over New York and the world gathered to see the ball drop from the Chemical Building, bringing in the New Year. There were many things to see in this area. He walked further west and was fascinated by the pornographic movie theatres and peep shows that were located on the block between 7th and 8th Avenues. Though it was still quite early in the morning, these store fronts had barkers in the doorways encouraging the persons walking by to enter their establishments for a fee. On 8th Avenue and 42nd Street, prostitutes were on the corner offering their services to men passing by. He was not sure if the prostitutes had been there all night or if they had just come out because it was now 10:30 am. This was the second time since he had been in New York that he had seen prostitutes on the street. The first time was the very same day he arrived from Santa Maria. He had seen them while the taxi traversed mid-Manhattan to deliver the Trinidadian businessman with whom he had shared the taxi ride from Kennedy Airport, to his destination.

No one from his family had come to Kennedy Airport to meet him upon his arrival. He had been told to take a cab from Kennedy Airport to 125th Street and Madison Avenue where his family lived, and his father owned a small cleaning store. He was not sure how to take a cab but was given the information that he would see the yellow cabs outside after he had gone through customs. He remembered the information which he had been given. First, he would go through immigration and then he would have to go through customs to determine if he was bringing anything illegal or anything that was not allowed such as fruits or local medicines from Santa Maria. He knew that family members always had lots of items to send to their relatives in New York. He had heard stories of persons who had their items confiscated from the custom officers. The people of Santa Maria are known for consuming a lot of tea. Not tea in tea bags that you would find in the supermarket but tea from a variety of herbs and local plants which are grown on the island. The most common plant used for making tea was the soursop. The tea made from the leaves of the soursop tree was very refreshing and said to be calming to the nerves. It was also said to be a plant which had cancer curing properties. The actual soursop, which is the fruit that the plant bears, was used to make a delicious drink. Another common bush tea was the sugar apple plant. He had both a sugar apple and a soursop tree in the backyard of the house where he lived with his aunt. Other common plants used to make bush tea were the moringa also called the 'Tree of Life', fever grass/lemon grass, nunu balsam and mint. All hot drinks consumed at breakfast were called tea by the local people of Santa Maria.

There is a story about a tourist in a local hotel who told a waitress that he wanted tea with his breakfast and the waitress proceeded to ask him what kind of tea he wanted. He repeated that he wanted tea, with the expectation that he would have been given a tea bag. The waitress also became frustrated and asked again what type of tea he wanted but this time she named the types of what she considered to be tea. She asked the tourist,

"What kind of tea do you want, coffee tea, Ovaltine tea, bush tea or Lipton tea?"

The tourist was puzzled and replied,

"Please, I will have the Lipton."

Many people from Santa Maria and other Caribbean islands arrived at Kennedy Airport in New York with bundles of leaves from various plants, intending to use them to make tea. This was so because these leaves were from tropical plants which did not grow in the cold climates of North America. Relatives living in the United States often requested these leaves from those leaving the islands. Often there were problems when customs officers found these items in the suitcases of those traveling from the Caribbean. The customs officers not knowing and not wanting to know what types of plants were being brought in, found it easier to simply confiscate the plants and to discard them. Testing the leaves to determine whether or not they were marijuana plants was too time consuming.

When Terrence arrived at the customs, he joined the line which was the shortest. The lady in front of him was also from Santa Maria and he looked closely when she was asked to open her suitcase for an inspection by a customs officer. The customs officer searched through her suitcase and the more he looked, it seemed that the more she had items that were questionable or inappropriate to bring into the United States. In one brown paper bag, she had ten Julie mangoes. Julie mangoes are very sweet and indeed delicious. On Santa Maria, it was not uncommon for a male suitor to tell a female that he was enamored with,

"Girl, you sweet like a Julie mango!"

That was a high compliment in Santa Maria, but the customs officer did not appear to be impressed with the Julie mangoes and they were confiscated. It was often said by those whose mangoes were confiscated that the customs officers later ate them.

The customs officer continued his search and dug deeper into her suitcase. She had fried fish wrapped in foil paper. Along with the fried fish, she had what was considered a delicacy in Santa Maria, ducana. Ducana was made from a mixture of white flour and sweet potatoes. The mixture was boiled after being wrapped in banana leaves. This was a dish from Ghana which survived the Atlantic crossing three hundred years before. The customs officer obviously would not have been interested in the origins and history of this tasty dish if she had told him and it too was taken away. Next, he found an abundance of plants to make 'bush tea'. These too were confiscated, perhaps the customs officer thought they were marijuana, or some other plant used as an intoxicant. He found other medicines commonly used in Santa Maria. There were bottles of Enos and Andrews Liver Salts. Also, there were bottles of Phensic, Ferol and Dettol. The seals on these bottles were not broken and she was allowed to keep them. Lastly, she had ten bottles of Cavalier Rum which was the locally brewed rum on the island. Six of those bottles were taken away because as a visitor, only four were allowed.

This customs inspection of the lady in front of him took longer than Terrence had anticipated but he did not mind waiting because he had been curious to see what was happening to his fellow passenger from Santa Maria. Next it was his turn and when asked, he said that he did not have anything to declare. He had been told to use those exact words to the customs officers. When asked if he was sure he had nothing to declare, he simply said yes. The customs officer directed him to place his suitcase on the counter and to open it. The customs officer then looked through the suitcase and seemed pleased that he did not find any fruits or leaves of plants for making tea. Terrence was sent on his way after the customs officer was satisfied that he had not brought any forbidden items into the United States.

As he exited the customs area, he saw hundreds of people there waiting to welcome their loved ones as they arrived from various places around the world. He had landed at the international terminal and it was full of people, more people than he had ever seen before. He looked around at all the people, but he did not expect to see any family members because he had already been told that there would be no one there to meet him and that he should take a taxi to Harlem.

Outside the terminal doors, he saw a line of yellow taxis waiting at the curb. Taxis in Santa Maria were not yellow, they were not painted in any specific color to identify them as taxis. They were essentially private cars operated by their individual owners as taxis. He also saw a line of people who were waiting to get taxis to take them to their destinations. He was happy to see that he was not the only one who had not been picked up by family members or friends. Seeing people lining up in an orderly fashion waiting for a taxi, on a first come first served basis, was also unusual for him because in Santa Maria people cut the lines and pushed to get ahead when any situation called for an orderly line up. There was no realization that it would have been so much easier to get on an orderly line instead of pushing and shoving to get served.

He walked over to the line of persons waiting to get a taxi. Immediately in front of him was a passenger from Trinidad who had been on the plane with him. The man recognized him from the plane and asked where he was going to and he answered that he was going to 125th Street in Harlem. The man then told him that he was also going to Manhattan and they could share a taxi. He agreed and they both entered the taxi and sat in the back seat. The Trinidadian had obviously done this before and took charge of the situation. He told the taxi driver that they were going to Manhattan and stated that he was going to 50th Street and 8th Avenue and that Terrence was going to Madison and 125th Street. He directed the taxi driver to take him to his destination first and Terrence would be next. As they drove to Manhattan, the Trinidadian struck up a conversation and told him that he was a businessman and that he visited New York quite often on business. Terrence was in awe of the tall buildings and was a bit distracted. He looked out the window and the expression on his face was one of wonder. After all, no building on Santa Maria was taller than a coconut tree. Now he was seeing buildings that appeared to kiss the sky. The Trinidadian told him that he would get used to seeing all the tall buildings and the multitude of people quite soon.

Terrence had not met many Trinidadians before, but he had heard of them. From his geography classes in high school, he learned that Trinidad was quite large compared to Santa Maria. He knew that Trinidad was the birthplace of 'calypso' and 'steel pan'. The Trinidadian calypso singers such as the Mighty Sparrow and Lord Brynner were famous throughout the West Indies. Trinidad was also the home and birthplace to some notorious criminals such as Manu Benjamin who reportedly blinded two sisters by stabbing them in the eyes with an icepick. Trinidad was also the birthplace of his favorite author, V.S. Naipaul. Naipaul had moved to England to attend Oxford University on an island scholarship. This was a prestigious award given to one student annually on the island. He had written several books which were becoming popular in the West Indies. *The Mystic Masseur* and *Miguel Street* explored life in Trinidad. In his travel book of the Caribbean called the *Middle Passage*, he used unflattering words to describe Santa Maria even though he had spent less than a day there as an in-transit passenger on his way to Jamaica.

When the taxi arrived at the destination requested by the Trinidadian, the taxi driver told him the fare that was on the meter and expected him to pay. The Trinidadian, in an assertive manner, told the taxi driver that he would not pay the fare directly to him but that he was giving the amount that was on the meter to Terrence, plus a tip and when he arrived at his destination, Terrence would pay him what was on the meter plus give him the tip. He was not sure what was happening, but the Trinidadian told him that taxi drivers often tried to collect a double fare by charging both of the passengers separately. The taxi driver was not pleased but the Trinidadian was adamant that the way he said the taxi driver would be paid was the way that it would be.

The taxi driver then drove east to Madison Avenue and turned left and headed north on Madison Avenue. On the way, the taxi driver did not speak. Terrence did not mind his quietness. It gave him a chance to continue to look out the window at the tall buildings that were taller than coconut trees and appeared to be kissing the sky. He was also fascinated with the large numbers of people on the streets compared to the small number of people on the streets of Santa Maria.

At 123rd Street and Madison Avenue, he saw a building which had a sign which said Hospital for Joint Diseases. That seemed odd and he wondered what exactly did the name of the hospital mean? Was it a hospital that cared only for people who had problems with their toes, fingers, knees and elbows? Opposite the hospital there was a park with a sign at the entrance that read Mount Morris Park.

The taxi crossed 125th street and the driver pulled over to the curb and got out of his taxi and put Terrence's suitcase on the sidewalk next to the telephone booth on the northwest corner.

"I am looking for 1958 Madison Avenue," he said to the taxi driver as he got out to speak with him.

The driver was nervous and decidedly uncomfortable. He was most definitely in a hurry to be on his way and said,

"You asked to go to 125th Street and Madison Avenue in Harlem and this is where you are, so this is it. You have to pay the fare which is on the meter."

At that moment, he heard his name being called from across the street. It was the voice of his brother who had been looking out for him from inside the dry cleaners that was owned by their father. His brother crossed the street, and he was no longer alone to deal with the taxi driver. He looked at the meter and paid the driver the amount that was on the meter and added the tip that was given to him by the businessman from Trinidad. The taxi driver got back into his taxi and sped off going north on Madison Avenue. He and his brother crossed the street and entered the cleaners. Next to the entrance of the cleaners, he noticed another entrance and above the entrance was painted 1958 Madison Avenue. This was the sign that he was looking for, but he did not see it at the time that the taxi stopped across the street and the driver put his suitcase on the sidewalk.

Terrence enjoyed walking around the area of Times Square by himself but decided that he would have lots of time to explore on subsequent trips to Manhattan. He retraced his steps to the IRT subway station at 42nd Street and took the number 7 train heading north to Harlem. He could have walked all the way to Grand Central Station, but he opted to take the train from Times Square instead. This was the train that would take him to 125th Street and Lennox Avenue. He had no difficulty getting on or off the train because the rush hour was over. There were characters on the train that he set about observing.

The most significant person that he observed on this day was a man who came from the adjacent subway car and immediately started to beg for spare change. This man was blind and had a walking stick that he swung from side to side. Passengers had to raise their feet when he was close to them to prevent him from hitting their feet as he walked by. He had a note written on a piece of cardboard attached to a string that hung from his neck. The writing, in bold letters on the piece of cardboard, stated,

"I am blind, please help, God Bless you, Thank you."

He was shabbily dressed and was unkempt. His shirt and pants were dirty and tattered. His hair was not combed, and he had a scraggly beard. In his right hand he held the walking stick that he swung and in his left hand he held an enamel cup in which the passengers placed coins or dollars. Each donation he received, he said,

"God Bless You."

Terrence's first instinct was to put some change into the blind man's cup, but he resisted and sat there just watching the blind man as he crossed and went into the next subway car. Several persons placed money into the blind man's cup and received blessings from him.

At 125th Street, Terrence exited the train, without any trouble and walked up the stairway to street level. Ahead of him, was someone who looked familiar. It was the blind man who had been begging on the train. He watched as the man folded his walking stick and removed the sign from around his neck. The man was walking without any trouble and he no longer needed the stick to maneuver. His eyes were wide open. The man was not blind at all.

As he walked, he caught up with the blind man. They were both going in the same direction towards 5th Avenue on 125th Street. He could not resist the urge to speak to the 'blind man' and said,

"You are the blind man from the train."

The 'blind man' looked at him as if he had been affronted and said,

"Mind your own fucking business."

He took the advice, which was more like an order, of the 'blind man' and headed home to 125th Street and Madison Avenue. He learned some valuable lessons that day on his venture to find employment with the airlines. The first lesson was that things were not always as easy as they appeared regarding what is printed in the want-ads section of the newspapers. Secondly, he learned that it was good to be a keen observer of what is taking place around you on the subway in particular and in New York City in general. This was particularly true when getting on and off a crowded subway car. Lastly, it was good to observe but it was not always good to get involved. Sometimes it was best to just observe and mind your own fucking business as the 'blind man' had told him.

◊◊

Chapter 2

It was with an illegal alien named Clem that Terrence made his second journey to mid-Manhattan to find a job. This time he had not seen the job in the classified section of the Sunday New York Times. He had not seen the job advertised anywhere. He had several friends who worked in the garment district in Manhattan. What they all had in common was that they had managed to leave Santa Maria and had managed to reach New York City without having the prerequisite documents to do so legally.

The route they took to arrive in New York City was a circuitous one. In the 1960's, times were difficult in Santa Maria. Times were doubly difficult if you did not have the benefit of a high school education. Many of the young men from Terrence's neighborhood left for the United States Virgin Islands where the pastures were believed to be greener. To their surprise, they also met difficult times in the Virgin Islands. Most often, they tried to settle in St. Thomas which was the more developed of the two larger Virgin Islands of St. Croix and St. Thomas. Tourism was developing in St. Thomas with the advent of hotels and cruise ships coming for daily stopovers. The lucky ones found work in the tourism sector as dishwashers in the hotels and others worked as waiters and bartenders. Others remained unemployed for long periods of time and depended on their friends who were barely getting by themselves. At the time, tourism was also developing in Santa Maria and some had previously held these same positions in local hotels. Often times, a young Santa Marian went to St. Thomas or St. Croix with a promise from a friend who had already migrated that he had a job waiting for him upon his arrival. Unfortunately, it was not unusual for a promise of assistance in this manner was made with no expectation that the person who made the offer would follow through. The offers were most often empty promises. Many travelled there with the offer in mind only to be told by the friend who made the offer that he was no longer able to help.

The room and board that was promised was withdrawn on their arrival. Some ended up sleeping in parks or with others in a similar situation who lived ten or more in a small apartment. They had to take turns to sleep. It was not unusual for one of the occupants of the overcrowded apartment to be awakened from the bed in which he was sleeping and told that he had to vacate the bed because his time was up, and it was the other person's turn to use the bed.

Upon their arrival in the Virgin Islands, they were granted permission by immigration officials to remain for two or three months. If they were successful in finding employment, their employer could petition the immigration department for their time to be extended in the form of a bond. For those who were unemployed and homeless, they were rounded up by immigration officers and deported back to Santa Maria. Upon their arrival back in Santa Maria, they never said that they had been deported. Lies abounded and the excuses for their return were plentiful. Anything ranging from a sick family member or not liking the Virgin Islands were reasons given. If they had managed to find employment in the Virgin Islands, most were satisfied with living there, but they knew that it was not their ultimate goal. Their ultimate goal was to make it to the mainland of the United States, notably New York City and specifically the Bronx, where most Santa Marians lived. If they did not find employment and managed to avoid deportation from the Virgin Islands, the next step would be to go to Puerto Rico. At the time, travelling from the Virgin Islands to Puerto Rico did not require a person to show any documents, it was tantamount to travelling from New York to Philadelphia. Those that made it to Puerto Rico were once again faced with the same obstacles which they faced in the Virgin Islands, but the difficulty was now compounded by the language barrier. Puerto Rico is the only United States territory where Spanish is the official language.

Many did make it to Puerto Rico. From Puerto Rico, it was their hope to make it to New York City. To get to New York City, they had to pretend to be from the Virgin Islands or from Puerto Rico. Of course, if they pretended to be Puerto Ricans, they had to be able to speak Spanish. Some could actually speak Spanish if they had lived there illegally for a period of time. The illegal aliens were often successful in purchasing the airline ticket to New York City and boarding the plane. Their difficulties arose once they were seated on the plane in Puerto Rico waiting for it to take off. The immigration officials knew that Puerto Rico was a gateway for those wishing to get to the mainland of the United States illegally, so the inspection procedures were increased. All the planes taking off to New York City were subject to an inspection by immigration officials. The inspection involved boarding the planes and inspecting the travel documents of selected passengers. Many were caught in this process but also many managed to evade the authorities and were successful in reaching to New York City.

There is a story about two illegals from Santa Maria who were traveling together from Puerto Rico to New York City. They were together, but to avoid suspicion they separated at the airport. They had travelled together to the airport and once they arrived, they feigned that they did not know each other. On the plane, one named Zee sat towards the front of the plane. The other named Nick sat towards the back. Nick did not have the opportunity to attend school in Santa Maria and he was illiterate in both Spanish and English. The story goes that while the inspectors were walking towards the back of the plane, they noticed that Nick had quickly picked up a magazine and pretended to be reading it. The magazine was actually being held upside down. When he was asked for his identification and travel documents, he admitted that he did not have the proper documentation. As he was being escorted from the plane and he reached the aisle where Zee was sitting, he said,

"See you later Zee, boy them catch me."

This of course caused the authorities to also ask for Zee's documents. They were both taken into custody and deported back to Santa Maria. A few years later they were successful in making their way to New York City, but they travelled separately on different days.

It was in this manner that Clem managed to be living in New York City, in the South Bronx. He had arrived with only the clothes on his back and was now working in the garment district in Manhattan. He told Terrence that he could get him a job working for the same company that he and another of their friends worked for. Terrence was curious and wanted to know what the job entailed but Clem was evasive about the functions required of the job but was quite confident that he could get him a job at the company for which he worked in the garment district.

Clem had told him that he worked in shipping, but he did not elaborate. Terrence had no idea what he meant when he told him that he worked in shipping. He did not know what the job entailed but Clem had assured him that the job was his if he wanted it. Terrence's was apprehensive because he remembered how he had been treated when he sought a position with the airlines. He was impressed by the way Clem walked into the building where he worked. He walked in with confidence and an air of self-importance. He walked as if he belonged.

The building was located at 35th Street and 7th Avenue in the heart of the garment district. As they walked through the revolving door and entered the building, Clem said,

"Don't be afraid man, the job is yours, just leave it to me. I will do the talking."

Terrence was not as confident as he had been when he went on his own to the Chrysler building to find a position with the Action Airline Employment Agency. His lack of confidence was on account of the fact that he was not wearing his only suit, the black sharkskin purchased by his sister for him to attend the funeral of his father that he did not really know. He had been told by Clem that he should not get dressed up. Additionally, he was not comfortable because he was applying for a job and did not know what was required of him in the position that Clem all but guaranteed that he would get. He was not confident because of his perceived mistreatment in his previous interview, and he did not like being told that he was not qualified for a position when he clearly met the required qualifications stipulated in the advertisement for the position.

The lobby was filled with people. Many of them were well dressed and appeared to be professionals. Terrence and Clem took the crowded elevator to the 7th floor. Even though they were in the back of the elevator they did not have any difficulty in getting out because as the elevator stopped, Clem simply asserted himself by pushing his way to the front. As the door opened, Clem got off and looked back to see that Terrence was behind of him. He placed his left foot in position to block the door so that it would not close before Terrence was able to get off. When they were in the lobby, Clem rebuked him by saying,

"Man, you have to be more aggressive when you are getting off the elevator, you sometimes have to push or they will not let you off, this nice boy thing don't work in New York. I know you were a nice boy back home but that don't work here."

The main reception office of the company was to the right, but they did not enter from the right, they entered a service door on the left. Upon entering, he observed that it was a warehouse filled with thousands of dresses. The dresses were all of different colors, styles, shapes and sizes. The dresses hung on metal poles. They walked through this area filled with dresses and came upon area another which was separated by a metal gate. Clem pushed a button located on the right side of the metal gate and a man on the other side pushed a button which gave a buzzing sound. This enabled the gate to be opened by giving it a push, which Clem did without hesitation. It was obvious that he had entered this gate, in this manner, many times before.

"Good Morning Mr. Weinstein,"

Clem said as he pushed the gate open and saw the man seated at the elevated counter. As Terrence walked in behind him, he continued,

"This is Terry, the guy I told you about, he is a very good worker."

"Good morning Mike, how are you doing, did you see the Mets last night? They lost again."

Mr. Weinstein did not acknowledge Terrence's presence but continued to talk about the baseball game of the previous night. Terrence stood there waiting until he was spoken to. He was not surprised to hear that Mr. Weinstein had referred to Clem as Mike because he had been told by Clem that he did not use his use real name on the job. His real name was not on his social security card. His social security card had the name Michael Carpenter.

Clem was using the social security card of a dead person, at least, that was what he had been told when he paid a man the five-hundred-dollar fee to obtain the social security card which would allow him to work in New York City.

Terrence also learned that the majority of his friends who were illegal aliens were working under assumed names and using social security cards which had the names of persons that they did not know.

There was a story about one of his friends who worked under an assumed name. At the end of his first week of work, the boss called him by the name on his social security card, the same name he had given them, expecting him to answer to give him his paycheck. The boss finally walked up to him and said, I have been calling you and you did not answer. His friend, whose real name was Kelvin John did not respond when the boss called him by the name he had used when he applied for the job.

All the other guys who had newly come to New York City from Santa Maria without proper documentation were told this story so that they could be aware not to make this same mistake. Clem had also coached Terrence regarding what should be said when he took him to meet Mr. Weinstein.

Clem had told him,

"Just tell him that your name is Terry, you don't have to use a fake name because you have your papers. You are straight."

Straight was the word that was used to indicate that someone had migrated legally to the United States. Clem went on,

"It's persons like me 'who came through the window' that have to be very careful with who we tell our names to. If the man asks you where you are from, you can say Santa Maria, but if he asks you where you know me from, you must say that you knew me when you lived in the Virgin Islands, St. Thomas to be exact but he probably won't ask you all that."

'Came through the window' was another way of describing the way illegal aliens entered the United States. As Terrence stood there waiting to be spoken to, Mr. Weinstein finally acknowledged his presence by asking,

"So, you are a good worker huh?"

"Yes," replied Terrence.

"Are you ready to work now?" Mr. Weinstein asked.

"Yes, I am," said Terry.

"Okay, well let's get you started."

Pointing to a several stacks of cloth that were piled high on push carts he said,

"Unload these carts that are here and make the piles like the others in the far corner."

The stacks in the far corner were piled high and almost touched the ceiling. The rolls of cloth were quite large. Each pushcart contained approximately twenty-five rolls.

Terrence realized what Mr. Weinstein wanted him to do. Even though he was not accustomed to this kind of manual labor, he did not hesitate. There were other piles of cloth which were stacked in the warehouse and this was what he was expected to do with the rolls of cloth on the pushcarts. He had hoped that he would have been doing something along the lines of what Clem said he was doing which was shipping. He was not sure exactly what was meant by shipping, but he reasoned that stacking rolls of cloth did not qualify as shipping.

He walked over to the first pushcart and pulled out a roll. He did not realize that it would have been so heavy, and it fell to the ground. The roll weighed approximately forty pounds. Clem was still there and witnessed what happened and he laughed out loud. This caused Terrence to be embarrassed and Clem saw his embarrassment and came over to lend a hand.

He quickly picked up a roll from the cart, and in one motion, placed it on the floor where the stack would be made. As he did this, he said to Terrence,

"What's the matter with you man? Just do it like this."

Clem pulled out a few more of the rolls of cloth and began making the stack on the floor. It was obvious Clem had made the stacks before. He then told Terrence that he would be back to pick him up for lunch. He left and went through the gate where they had been buzzed in by Mr. Weinstein. He went to the first area that they came in after they had gotten off the elevator, the area that had been filled with dresses of all types. He was glad that Clem had left because even though he was responsible for getting him the job, he wanted to be able to handle the responsibilities on his own. He was also quite more reserved than Clem and he was uncomfortable with his forthrightness.

Terrence continued to unload the pushcarts. By the time he was finished, he was told to load the same pushcarts with other rolls of cloth that had already been stacked up almost to the ceiling. He found it easier to load the pushcarts than to unload them to make the stacks because while making the stacks the entire stack could fall to the ground. Shortly after he had restacked the pushcarts, three other workers arrived to take them away. Mr. Weinstein stated that the workers were from the shipping department. These restacked rolls were shipped out to the company that would make the dresses. Terrence then realized what Clem had meant when he said that he worked in shipping. He had to deliver dresses or rolls of cloth to other areas of the garment district. Shipping was the umbrella term used to describe just about every aspect of working in the warehouse of a dress manufacturing company in the garment district of Manhattan.

The situation was confusing to Terrence. Stacks of cloth were continuously brought in which had to be unloaded into neat piles. On the other hand, he was also required to restack the pushcarts which were then picked up. Mr. Weinstein counted the rolls of cloth as they came in, he was also sure to count the rolls of the restacked rolls of cloth when the workers left with them. It was later on that he realized that the rolls of cloth came in from suppliers and had to be stored until the dressmakers were ready for them, then they were shipped out accordingly.

After unloading and loading these rolls of cloth for two hours, Terrence grew tired and started looking at his watch wishing that it was lunch time, but it was only 10:00am. He had been working for only two hours, but it seemed to him that he had been working for a much longer period. Lifting the heavy rolls of cloth was taxing and he was not accustomed to this type of manual labor. It was taking its toll on him. He was exhausted.

◊◊

Chapter 3

Only a couple of months before, he was in high school. As a student, he did not always do well. The secondary school that he attended was a combination middle school and high school. In his middle school years, he was lost and had no direction. He went to school daily but there was no one to direct him to put him on the path that could lead to success in school. His mother had died when he was six years old, and he and his siblings had been abused and abandoned by their father. At six, he was too young to understand the gravity of this and how it would affect his life. The memories of his mother were etched in his young mind. One day she was there caring for him and the next day she was gone. She died at the hands of a negligent doctor. This doctor was a part of a medical system that did not hold doctors responsible for their actions. This type of system was pervasive in the Caribbean. It is the system that V.S. Naipaul describes in his early novel, *The Mystic Masseur*, about Trinidadian life and by extension life in the Caribbean islands. It was a system of neglect as opposed to accountability when dealing with the medical needs of the poor.

She went to the hospital for a simple operation which was specific to females and she died leaving six children with no father. She had been diagnosed as suffering from fibroids and told that it was necessary to have surgery to remove them. The expectation was that she would have the surgery performed in the hospital by a local doctor and she would return home in a matter of a week or two. The doctor who performed the surgery botched it and Terrence's mother bled to death. He remembers the night of his mother's death. He was at his aunt's home during the time that his mother was hospitalized.

The day that she left for the hospital, she had told him that she would be going to the hospital and that she would be back soon. He remembers her packing a small suitcase and getting into the car that took her to the hospital. It was about four in the afternoon. Later he and his siblings walked to the home of his aunt. Several nights later he was awakened by his aunt in the middle of the night and told that his mother had died. He did not yet understand the concept of death as permanent, and he went back to sleep. The next day was somber with people coming and going. He returned to their home and remembers that they had brought the body of his mother to their home. She was lying on a piece of wood in the living room and the piece of wood was supported by two chairs, one on either end. Beneath his mother's body was a slab of ice which gave the room a cold feeling. No one talked to him about what was happening, and he did not ask. In the morning, on the day of the funeral, several people came to the house. He watched as his aunts and other female relatives prepared his mother for her funeral. A white dress was put on her and her hair was combed. A hearse arrived and waited in the street in front of the house. A wooden coffin was removed from the hearse and brought into the house. His mother's body was placed into the coffin and moved to the front yard, where it was once again propped up on two chairs. The coffin was opened, and Terrence and his siblings were asked to stand next to the coffin and pictures were taken. After the pictures were taken, the coffin was closed and placed into the hearse for the journey to the church for the funeral service. Terrence did not realize it, but it was the last time that he would see the face of his mother.

His mother's funeral took place during Carnival. The funeral procession marched up Temple Street past the house where he would later live with his aunt who took them in after the abuse meted out by their father after his return from Curacao. As the procession passed the house of his aunt, he saw his cousin, who was at one of the windows, lower his head because he could not bear to see the funeral procession of his aunt pass by. He had not attended the funeral because he was too distraught. Now he could not bear to see the funeral procession of his aunt pass by on the way to Anglican Cathedral of St. John the Divine which sits on a promontory overlooking the capital city. One block away from the cathedral, the procession ran into the Carnival parade of people dancing in the streets. Carnival was supposed to be a celebration in commemoration of the abolition of slavery on August 1st, 1834.

After the service at the church, the funeral procession then headed to the public cemetery where another shorter service took place. This service consisted of a few prayers and the singing of hymns. At the gravesite, he remembers standing alone behind the crowd as the grave diggers lowered the wooden coffin bearing the remains of his mother into the grave. After the coffin was put into the grave, the grave diggers then set about with their shovels to fill the grave with the dirt which had been dug from the grave and the service came to an end.

Later as a high school senior, Terrence noticed a bump on the left side of his neck. He was taken to the same doctor who had botched his mother's surgery. The doctor told him and his sister who had taken him that he had a gland which had become swollen from being strained. The doctor recommended surgery to remove it and Terrence declined. Terrence said that he did not want to have it removed by the doctor and asked to be taken to another doctor. Before the appointment was made to see another doctor, the swelling on his neck went down and never came back.

Terrence had a father, but he was not a part of his life. At the time of his mother's death, his father was living and working in the Dutch Caribbean island of Curacao and did not return for the funeral of his wife. He returned years later, but Terrence was not certain of the time or his own age when he first met his father.

He knows for sure that he had never met him up to the time of his mother's death when he was six years old. He does not recall meeting him when he was in primary school, so he reasoned that it must have been in his first or second year of his middle school years at ten or eleven years of age. Their first meeting was unusual. One afternoon he had been outside playing with friends in the neighborhood and one of his sisters came and called him and said that he had to come home. On the way, his sister told him that their father was at home and that he had just arrived from Curacao. At the house, he met a man and was told that the man was his father. The man did not reach out to hug him and they made no physical contact. He said hello and stood to the side while his sisters spoke to the man, the man whom he had been told was his father.

In the days that followed, his father set about turning their small living room into a tailor shop. The living room turned tailor shop became a gathering place for his father's friends. On the weekends, their living room doubled as a tailor shop and a rum drinking shop. This is where his father's friends gathered to talk and get drunk.

His father brought no stability to his life and to the lives of his siblings. The situation did not feel normal. A man had come into his life who was supposed to be his father, but never having a father before, he did not know what it meant. The dynamics in the house were dysfunctional in general but on the weekends the dynamics degenerated from dysfunctional to border on abuse and torture. During the week, his father did his work as a tailor in the living room. The persons who came to the house to see his father during the week were customers who wanted to have various items made. The usual requests were for pants and or suits. Terrence would notice his father measuring and writing down the measurements of the persons requesting pants or suits to be made for them. He wrote all the measurements down in a black and white notebook. Apparently, he was good at being a tailor because he had many customers and in a short period of time had rebuilt a good clientele. Many of his customers were people that he had made clothes for before he moved to Curacao. When they had heard that he was back, they came back to him for his services. The living room filled up with cloth of all kinds and with finished suits and pants hanging on make-shift racks to be collected by persons who had brought them in to be made.

On Friday afternoons, his father's friends came by and most often each one came bringing rum. It was not unusual for four or five of his friends to be in the living room with him at this time. He would be doing his tailoring and drinking rum with them. Soon he would stop doing his tailoring and they all would be drinking rum. From time to time, all the rum bottles were empty, and they would send out to buy more and the drinking would resume. This would go on until late into the Friday night, when his father's friends left.

At other times, his father would leave home with his friends and continued drinking at another location. Sometimes he would go to another friend's house or to the local rum shop. In Santa Maria, bars were also called rum shops, because alcohol could be bought and consumed at these locations. His father would manage to make it home in a drunken state late into the night usually well after midnight.

On Saturdays, his father's friends started coming to the house in the mornings and the drinking started then and continued all day and into the night. The weekends were the worst times and when his father came home drunk late at night. It was most terrifying to Terrence and his siblings.

Their father would come home drunk and shortly after he entered the house he would begin to curse. The older ones were usually up and waiting for him to come home to begin his tirade of cursing and yelling and talking about perceived wrongs that had been done to him during the course of his life.

Here was a man who had fathered at least twelve children, six with his wife and six before he married and did not take care of or act like a real father to any of them. Now in his drunken state, he often talked about how he had been wronged and misunderstood.

Shortly after the tirades began, all the children would be awakened. He would tell all of them to get out of his house. All six would leave the house through the back door and gather in the backyard shivering in fright and wondering what to do next. This happened usually around two in the morning. All the children would then make the trek from their home to the home of their aunt who lived about half a mile away. They went to their aunt's home with only the clothes on their backs.

On Sunday evenings, after he had slept off the alcohol, he would come to their aunt's home and ask the children to come back. The children would return, not because they wanted to but because they felt that it was their duty to do so because he was their father, and their options were limited because they did not envision that they had a viable alternative. Being so young, Terrence had no choice in the matter of returning. He did not want to return but he went back with the others.

He was not afraid of his father. He was somewhat detached from the situation. It was similar to the experience he had when his mother had died a few years before, he did not understand what was going on. At the funeral of his mother he did not cry, though he saw others crying and wailing profusely. He had the ability not to show his emotions in circumstances which were difficult. It was not willful, it was just that he did not fully understand the gravity of the circumstances and even if he did understand it, there was nothing that he could do to change it.

It all came to a head on the weekend after Terrence's second oldest sister had come out of the hospital after having an emergency appendectomy. She had spent two weeks in the hospital and returned home on the Thursday before the incident which took place early Sunday morning. Their father returned home at 2:00am after one of his usual Saturday night drunken binges. He proceeded to yell and blame others for perceived slights that he had endured during his life. In the process, he picked up a horse whip which he kept next to his bed and attempted to hit his daughter who had just come out of the hospital three days before. Terrence's older brother stopped him from hitting her by standing in front of her and prevented his hand from coming down after he had raised his hand in the air to deliver the blow.

After the father was stopped, he began to cry and stated that his son had beaten him up, when in fact no such thing happened. The six children once again gathered in the backyard and proceeded to walk to their aunt's house. On the way, they decided that they would not return to their father's house. That Sunday when he came to pick them up, the second oldest sister, the one who had the recent appendectomy, and for whom the blows from his horse whip were intended, told him that they would not return.

It was also at this time that Terrence knew that he would never be an alcoholic. He made the decision after he had witnessed the negative effects that alcohol had on his father. He viewed alcohol as poison in a bottle. It had to be poison or worse. He knew that there was something in a rum bottle that could make a man abuse and abandon his kids. He knew that there was something in a rum bottle which caused him great pain and he was determined to control the demons in the bottle. He would control them by never drinking alcohol.

Terrence never spoke to his father again until he migrated to the United States. Truth be told, he does not remember speaking to him during the time that his father returned from Curacao and he turned their living room into a tailor shop and rum drinking shop and routinely terrorized and abused him and his siblings.

He spoke to his father only once from the time of his arrival in New York City to the time of his father's death from prostate cancer six weeks later. Up to the time of this man's death, the man that he was told was his father, he had never once referred to him as Dad or Daddy as most fathers were called or referred to in Santa Maria. The subconscious pain which this man had caused Terrence negated any normal paternal bonds which could have developed between father and son.

The taxi driver who had driven him to Harlem had put him out of the taxi on the corner of 125th Street and Madison Avenue and raced off. He was obviously not comfortable being in Harlem and wanted to get out of there as fast as he could.

Fortunately, his brother had been looking out for him and saw him as he got out of the taxi. His suitcase had already been put on the sidewalk by the taxi driver. He and his brother crossed the street and entered the cleaners which was owned by their father. He already knew that they lived upstairs on the fourth floor of the building and the cleaners was on the street level. Shortly after his arrival, they went upstairs and saw one of his two sisters who lived in the apartment with his father and brother. The other sister, the one who was the victim of their father's wrath on that fateful night when they decided not to return to live with him was at work. Upon entering the apartment, he was ushered into the room where his father was lying on the bed barely recognizable. Prostate cancer had wreaked havoc on his body and he was a skeleton. It appeared that he weighed at maximum no more than 115 pounds. He said hello to his father and left the room to unpack his suitcase. Seeing his father in this condition, he felt neither anger nor pity. He knew that it was only a matter of time before his father would die. He looked more dead than alive. In the weeks that followed, he avoided going into his father's room to see him or to speak to him. On one occasion, the ambulance had to be called to take him to the hospital. The cancer had metastasized and had spread to virtually all the bones in his body making them extremely brittle. On this day, his father simply tried to use his arms to help himself to sit up in bed and the extra pressure snapped the bone in his upper left arm. The ambulance came and took him to the hospital where his left arm was put in a sling and he was brought back home in the ambulance. He was unable to walk, so he was taken back and forth on a stretcher.

The doctors who attended to him said that there was nothing they could do. They said that he would be dead in a matter of weeks if not days.

A day or two after this incident where he broke the bone in his left arm by trying to use his arms to sit up, Terrence went into his father's room and spoke to him. It is the only time in his life that he remembers having a conversation with his father. He initiated the very brief conversation. Terrence simply said to his father, who was in his bed with his left arm in a sling, near death,

"Why didn't you take care of us when we needed you?"

His father looked at him and turned his head away, and said,

"If I was well, you would not ask me that question."

Terrence thought, 'Oh how I wish that you were well so that you could answer my question.' Once again, his father was robbing him of an opportunity to get answers to questions which he needed to understand about his own life and the life of his father. Terrence felt no anger or pity for this man that he did not know. Terrence simply left the bedroom where his father lay dying from the prostate cancer that had ravished his body. Terrence was not sure if his father was capable of regret or if he was ashamed of the way he had acted as a father.

A week later he died. The second oldest sister, the one who would have been the recipient of the blows from the horsewhip if his brother had not stopped his father, had gone into his room and spoke to him but she got no response. He had died some time during the night and his body was now stiff and he was unresponsive to his daughter who had come into the room to look after his needs.

The New York Police Department was notified that there was a death at the house and a police officer came to the house to ensure that there was no foul play which caused the death. An hour later, a medical doctor came to the house and pronounced him dead. The undertaker whose business was located on 125th Street and Park Avenue, a few steps away from the train which took people to Mamaroneck and Scarsdale, came to the house and placed the body in a brown body bag and zipped it shut. They then took his father's body away.

Terrence continued to unload the carts and make the piles in the warehouse and also restacked the pushcarts. It was tedious and he was relieved when the time came and Clem arrived to get him for lunch.

He asked Clem to wait for him because he had to use the restroom to wash his hands and face which were covered in dust and dirt. The dust and dirt which now covered him had accumulated on the rolls of cloth in the warehouse. His clothes were clean when he arrived, now dust and dirt were all over him and on his clothes. When he exited the restroom, Clem was there waiting and told him to hurry up because they only had thirty minutes for lunch. Terrence thought that they would have had an hour which was the norm. Even in school in Santa Maria, the students had an hour for lunch.

When they left, Terrence noticed that they were going to a different elevator than the one they used when they arrived in the morning. It was clear that this elevator was different, and it was not as clean and well-kept as the others. He was told that this was the service elevator, and this is the one they would be using in the future. This elevator also had an elevator operator who moved a series of levers to get it going. It appeared old and rickety when compared to the one used in the morning.

The restaurant that they went to for lunch was located on 35th Street. It was filled with other workers from the garment district. The cooks and servers seemed to know all the customers on a first name basis. They sat at the counter and Clem was served a beef stew with rice. Clem introduced Terrence to the servers as his friend and instructed them to serve him the same thing. The food was terrible and barely edible. Terrence ate a quarter of what was put on his plate and left the rest. Even the soda which came out of a fountain did not taste like the other sodas to which he had been accustomed. It tasted like a mixture of water and sugar. It reminded of a drink he had when he was a little boy called sugar water. It was made by simply mixing brown sugar from the factory at Gunthropes and water. He had a few sips and left the remainder on the counter. After Clem expressed a few more pleasantries with other workers who were in the restaurant, it was time to return to work.

Back upstairs at work, Terrence continued with the tasks he had been working on all morning. At the end of the workday at 5:00pm, he was exhausted and looked forward to going home where he could get clean and get some needed rest.

At home, he was asked about the job and he responded by saying that it was okay and that it was a lot of work. He did not wish, at that time, to try to explain that he was working in the garment district in a warehouse filled with rolls of cloth and dresses.

He also knew that he would not last very long in this job. From all indications, there was not much of a chance for any upward mobility, and it did not fit into his overall plan of getting a college education and becoming what he considered to be successful in life.

Clem and several of his friends who had been living in NYC for at least two years before Terrence, worked in the garment district and he did not think that they had made sufficient progress towards being successful. Yes, they were earning a living, but Terrence did not see this as a career job. They were barely existing from paycheck to paycheck. They were in no financial position to help their family members back in Santa Maria. All of his other friends who had remained in Santa Maria had managed to secure jobs with the airlines upon graduation from high school and had the benefit of being able to travel at substantially reduced costs if they had to pay at all. One of his cousins who worked for the local airline, already had a job lined up for him upon graduation if he had stayed in Santa Maria. The job went instead to his next-door neighbor who was one of Terrence's friends.

The next day, Terrence was back at it again doing the same thing with the large rolls of cloth, unpacking pushcarts and making huge stacks, then restacking the pushcarts with other rolls of cloth which had to be delivered to the dress making factory.

After doing this for a few days, Terrence expressed his reservations about the job to Clem and was told that he should be patient because things would get better. He was told that if he was patient, he would be able to make extra money on the side. Terrence did not know how he would be making extra money from this job because it was not a job where money was exchanged.

Each night that Terrence went home, there was not much that he could do other than to take a shower, have dinner and then go to bed. The job was exhausting, and he was too tired to do anything else.

One day during the next week, Mr. Weinstein called Terrence to come over to his elevated desk. Terrence went over and to his surprise, Mr. Weinstein said to him,

"Can you count?"

Because he was surprised and startled by the question, he said,
"Excuse me?"

Mr. Weinstein, repeated the question,

"Can you count?"

Terrence was now sure that he had heard the question correctly
and responded,
"I graduated from high school."

Mr. Weinstein then said in a stern voice,

"I did not ask you if you graduated from high school, I asked
you if you could count."

Terrence wondered if it was possible to graduate from high
school in New York City without being able to count. Then, still
smarting that he had been asked what to him was an obvious
question, he responded,

"Yes, I can count."

Then Mr. Weinstein, said,

"Go over to the other side, they need help counting the
dresses over there."

Mr. Weinstein pressed the buzzer and he exited to the other side
to the area where Clem worked in 'shipping.' He learned a
valuable lesson by this interaction with Mr. Weinstein. He

learned that in the U.S., to a certain extent, no one cared about you or your accomplishments. He also learned that sometimes it is just best to answer the immediate question that is asked and to answer only yes or no if that is what the question required.

He went to the other side and was greeted by another man who had a position with the company that was similar to the one that Mr. Weinstein had. He said to Terrence,

"Mr. Weinstein told me that you graduated from high school, I want you to count the dresses on these two rows, but I want you to separate them into bunches of fifty."

All the dresses had to be counted but he had to place a marker to separate them. Mr. Weinstein had called the man to tell him that Terrence would be coming over to help with the counting and in the process told him that Terrence was a high school graduate. Terrence was now unsure if it was an advantage or a disadvantage for him to be a high school graduate in this situation. The fact that Mr. Weinstein told the supervisor in the warehouse that he was a high school graduate seemed to indicate that it might be an advantage. He knew that Clem and the other illegals that worked for the company were not high school graduates, but he also knew that they were able to count. He would later learn that the company had about forty employees who were in the same position as he was. They carried out several duties which did not require high school graduation as a prerequisite to being effective. He found out that some were unable to read and write and unlikely able to count as well. Their jobs required them to perform the manual duties such as unloading pushcarts and stacking rolls of cloth in the warehouse. Others made deliveries of dresses to department stores. This required them to push large quantities of dresses which were stacked on a rack with wheels, on the street, from their location to any place in the garment district they were sent.

There were two types of equipment with wheels used to deliver dresses from one place to the next. The first was a dress rack with wheels and the next was a box truck. The box truck was simply a box on wheels with the opening on the top. Protruding from the box was a bent metal pole on which dresses could be hung. The box truck was used by one individual to make a delivery of forty dresses or less. The racks with wheels could hold up to one hundred dresses each. These required two workers to handle them, one person to steer them from the front and another person to push them from the back.

He had been sent to make deliveries like this and he did not like being out on the street pushing racks and box trucks around the garment district. Sometimes this required him to be pushing the carts on 34th Street to make deliveries to Macy's, one of the largest and most famous stores in the world. He did not want to be seen by people from Santa Maria while he was pushing dresses on the street. In Santa Maria, he would have been working for an airline and here, where he had ostensibly gone to better himself, he was pushing dresses on the street.

It was from making deliveries using the box truck that extra money could be made. He found out from Clem how this was done. It was really stealing, and he was most uncomfortable when he was involved in stealing a number of dresses from the company. He was required to deliver forty dresses to a store on 40th Street and 8th Avenue. The dresses were counted out and hung on the steel pipe of the box truck but before he left to deliver them, Clem placed an additional ten dresses at the bottom of the box truck where they could not be seen. He was told to drop them off to a man at a store on 39th street between 7th and 8th Avenues. He delivered the stolen dresses as directed. Later, after work that day, he walked with Clem to the store where he had earlier delivered the stolen dresses and witnessed Clem receive fifty dollars for the ten stolen dresses. Clem gave him twenty-five dollars which he reluctantly accepted. Clem justified the stealing by saying that the company worked them very hard and did not adequately compensate them for the work they did. Even though Terrence agreed with Clem's assessment, he was uncomfortable with stealing and did not want to be a part of it. He asked Clem not to put any dresses in the bottom of the box truck in the future if he was the one doing the delivery. Clem agreed but he was uncomfortable with what Terrence had said to him. Terrence was a proud person and did not want to embarrass himself and his family by stealing dresses from his employer.

It was this pride that he managed to develop while living in the Caribbean that almost got him seriously hurt while he worked for this company in the garment district. The workers were not well educated, and they often made fun of each other and also the workers who were foreign born were made fun of by the native-born Americans. It was not unusual to hear the native-born Americans refer to the foreign born as monkeys. One day as he was counting dresses, he was asked a question by a fellow worker who was an American born in the South. He had a pronounced southern accent. Terrence spoke with his distinct Caribbean accent. Terrence's maternal grandmother, Aunt Kitty, had lived in New York City for almost fifty years and she also spoke with her distinct Caribbean accent which she was proud of. This native-born fellow employee, who in all probability had felt the sting of southern discrimination for most of his life, now decided to have fun at Terrence's expense, after he answered the question which he had been asked, this person said,

"Why don't you speak English?"

He responded,

"I am speaking English."

Then to take it a step further, the native-born American from the South said,

"You call that shit English? They should teach you mother fuckers to speak English before you ride over here on the banana boat."

Terrence should have ignored the ignorant statement but instead he chose to respond by saying,

"Yeah, I came over here riding on a banana boat and when I was riding on the banana boat, your sister was riding on my banana."

This response angered the native-born American from the South and he threatened to beat his 'ass' right there. Fortunately, there were other workers who stopped him from assaulting Terrence. He was told that it was his fault because he is the one who started with the insults. After this incident, they both kept their distance from each other. There was no doubt in Terrence's mind that if the other co-workers had not interceded, he would have been seriously injured by this person, who was older and physically twice his size. Ironically Terrence had never seen a banana boat. In fact, Terrence had flown to New York City on a jet aircraft and had actually sat in the cockpit of the aircraft with the three pilots for about thirty minutes. Because he was travelling alone, he was put in first class by a family friend who worked for the airline. Every time the flight attendant went into the cockpit to serve the pilots, Terrence would stretch himself out from his seat and try to look into the cockpit. The flight attendant saw that Terrence did this a couple of times. After observing his actions, he noticed that she turned around and went back into the cockpit. She then came out and told him that the captain said that he could come into the cockpit to sit with them. She then escorted him into the cockpit and introduced him to the captain who sat on the left. Terrence sat in the empty chair behind the captain. One pilot sat in the right seat next to the captain and the third pilot was sitting in the seat next to the one in which Terrence sat. The first thing Terrence observed as he sat down was that none of the pilots had their hands on the steering wheels. He knew that in order to properly drive a car, the driver's hand had to be on the steering wheel, if not the car would quickly go off course causing an accident. He immediately asked the pilot why they were not steering the plane and was told that they did not have to steer it manually because it was on automatic pilot and that they only had to hold on to the wheel when they were landing. Terrence was in awe that they were not even looking through the windshield of the plane to ensure that the plane was going in the right direction. After about thirty minutes, he thanked the captain for allowing him to sit in the cockpit and returned to his seat. Terrence was not sure that if he had told his coworker that he sat in the cockpit of a Boeing 727 on the way to New York City that it would have changed his mind about kicking his ass. The guy was just looking to bully someone smaller than he was, and Terrence did not feel like backing down.

There was another incident that occurred which Terrence thought was funny and embarrassing at the same time. Another man from Santa Maria came to work for the company at which Terrence was employed. Terrence had met him only once before. They were not friends. On the first assignment of his employment, he was sent to deliver dresses to a department store. It was not a typical delivery of simply delivering dresses which had been ordered by the department store. This time, the new employee was required to accompany one of the salesmen to make a sales pitch to one of the buyers at the department store. He started to work at 8:00am that morning and he was immediately given a large clothes bag with twenty dresses and told to accompany the salesman to his destination. The salesman was dressed in a suit, which gave him an air of professionalism and the worker was dressed in a shirt, jeans and tennis shoes. As they exited the building on 7th Avenue, the salesman made a right and the worker followed him. The salesman did not speak to the worker with the dresses in the bag, he simply walked at a brisk pace with the expectation that the worker would keep pace behind him. This was the normal procedure when workers accompanied the salesmen to show the new collection of dresses and to make their sales pitches. By the time the salesman reached 40th Street and 7th Avenue, he looked back to ensure that the worker was still keeping pace but to his surprise the worker was nowhere in sight. The worker had disappeared into the crowd. Thinking that the worker was simply unable to keep up with him, he waited for a few minutes, but the worker still did not catch up. The salesman now thought that he could simply walk back to the offices of the company and the worker would be there and he would have chastised him and told him that he should keep pace. Once again, the worker was nowhere to be found. There was a thought that maybe the worker had become lost, and he might show up later in the morning but that did not happen either.

Days later, Clem told Terrence that he had seen the worker in the Bronx and the worker had told him that the salesman was a damn fool. The worker asked why the salesman would walk away from him with the dresses and they did not even know each other. The worker said that he simply took the twenty dresses that were in the bag and sold them for ten dollars each. He had made $200 for walking less than five blocks up 7th Avenue. He went looking and found another job a week later in the garment district a few blocks away. The dresses were the new design which the salesman had hoped that the department stores would buy in large quantities.

Terrence worked at this job for one month before quitting. There was a specific incident which caused him not to return to work for this company in the garment district. For several days, he and the other workers were required to work overtime. They were not asked to work overtime, they were told. There was no time limit for them to leave, they were told when they could leave. On consecutive nights they were given permission to leave at 9:00pm. Considering that they only had thirty minutes for lunch, and they worked without breaks, this made for long and tiring days.

On the third night, Terrence was exhausted and did not feel like working until 9:00pm. The situation was not made any better when the supervisors ordered food for their dinner but did not order or offer any dinner to the workers. At 7:00pm Terrence decided that he had had enough, he was going home. As he walked by the desk of the supervisor, he was stopped and asked,

"Where are you going?"

"I am going home," was his response.

The supervisor then said,

"There is lots of work to be done, you will go when I tell you that you can go."

Terrence found it odd that the supervisor was saying this to him when he himself was sitting at his desk eating the dinner that was delivered for him by a runner from a nearby restaurant. Terrence looked at him with no expression on his face and said,

"I am hungry like you are, please buzz the gate, so that I can leave."

The supervisor was surprised by his forthrightness and calm demeanor. He buzzed the gate open, and Terrence left. It was his last day working in the garment district. He went home and told his family members that he was out of a job, he simply said that he did not like how he was being treated and that he would not go back to that place to work. In the short time that he had worked there, he had learned some valuable life lessons and he had also learned some of the nuances of being a Caribbean immigrant in New York City.

◊◊

Chapter 4

Terrence's sister had married a man from Santa Maria. It was some time after she had stopped working for her father in the cleaners. Their father had migrated to the United States and remarried. His new marriage was to a lady that he had known in Santa Maria who had migrated to New York City several years before. Getting married to this lady, who was in possession of her green card, also qualified him to get his green card. The marriage did not last very long, but he got his green card in the process. His children had heard that he had remarried but they never gave it much thought. He was not a part of their lives after they refused to come back to live with him after the fateful night when he had tried to beat one of his daughters with a horsewhip. It was difficult for them to forgive him for trying to beat his daughter with a horsewhip shortly after she had been hospitalized. She had just undergone an appendectomy and was recovering at home.

After moving to New York City, he got a job as a tailor in a dry-cleaning store on 5th Avenue between 125th Street and 126th Street in Harlem. At the time, he lived in a kitchenette several blocks north of the cleaners on 5th Avenue. A kitchenette could be described as a small room with a tiny kitchen. Bathroom facilities were in the hallway and were communal with the other two tenants on the floor.

Living close by was a good idea because he could walk back and forth to work, thus saving the money he would have had to spend commuting. His employer owned two dry cleaning stores, one on 5th Avenue and the other on Madison Avenue. His employer decided to sell his dry-cleaning store on Madison Avenue, and Terrence's father scraped together the money to buy it. The store was very small, and the workspace could barely fit two people. There was an area for a tailor to work on a sewing machine and small area for a person to work as a cashier and to take in the clothes which were brought in by customers to be cleaned or repaired.

The storage area for the clothes which were cleaned was quite small and compact. The dry cleaning was not done at the store, it was done by a dry-cleaning company in the Bronx. Clothes to be cleaned were picked up each morning by 10:00am and delivered by 5:00pm that very same afternoon.

During negotiations to purchase the store, Terrence's father called his second oldest daughter with his deceased wife and asked her if she would leave Santa Maria to come to work for him in the cleaners that he was in the process of purchasing. Other than having a job in New York City, he promised that he would file her papers so that she would get her green card, thus enabling her to live permanently in the United States. At the time, it was not difficult for parents to sponsor their children under the family reunification goals of the United States Immigration Department. The offer seemed like a good one for her, but she decided that this was an opportunity for her to negotiate for all of her siblings, who were still living in Santa Maria, to move to New York City. Two siblings had moved to New York City in the early sixties to live with their grandmother, Aunt Kitty. They had moved several years earlier to live with their grandmother who had migrated to New York City during the great migration to the United States in the early 1920's. Their grandmother had come by steamship and had gone through Ellis Island like the hundreds of thousands of European immigrants from places such as Italy, Ireland, England and Scandinavia. She sent for them and the two entered the United States on visas as visitors and then applied for and received student visas which allowed them to remain longer in the United States while they attended school.

She told her father that she would be willing to move to the United States to work in his dry cleaners on the condition that he filed the papers for all of them who were still living in Santa Maria at the time. He agreed and she moved to New York City to live with him and to work for him. She came on a visitor's visa because the permanent resident visa would have taken at least a year to be completed. It was easier for her to come on a visitor's visa and then for him to file for her permanent residency while she was already in New York City.

Things were going well when she first came. They rented a four-bedroom apartment on the fourth floor in the same building with the cleaners. Once again money was saved because there was no commute to work except for walking up and down four flights of stairs.

After the older brother and youngest sister came a year later, she left the cleaners and a took a job working for the American Telephone and Telegraph company also more commonly known as AT&T. The headquarters of this company was located on Canal Street and Avenue of the Americas also known as 6th Avenue. She worked at a satellite office on 48th Street and Park Avenue as a tele-typist.

Shortly after her arrival, he had become ill and had been diagnosed with prostate cancer. The prognosis given by his doctors was that he was unlikely to survive for a long period of time and that he would live for at most two years if that much. Her duties in the cleaners were taken over by the youngest sister and oldest brother. She took this job to ensure that there was money coming in other than from the cleaners.

After her wedding, she received several wedding gifts from her co-workers which were large in size. She asked Terrence to meet her one day at the time she got off from work in order to help her to bring home the gifts. That afternoon, he found his way to the office where his sister worked. While there, he was introduced to her co-workers and also her supervisor. Her supervisor asked her if Terrence was working, and she said that he was not currently working but he was looking for a job. The supervisor gave Terrence a letter of introduction and told him to go to the main office at 32 Avenue of the Americas and ask for a Ms. Jones in the personnel office.

On the Monday of following week, he dressed again in his one and only suit, the black sharkskin bought for him by his sister to attend the funeral of their father. After getting off the number four express on Canal Street, he walked west for two blocks and found the building. The building was quite imposing and took up the entire block. He walked through the main doors and was in the lobby, which had an extremely high ceiling. The personnel office was located in the far-right hand corner of the lobby. He walked into the office and went to the desk of the receptionist and asked for Ms. Jones. Her name was written on the envelope which he had been given by the supervisor of his sister. The receptionist asked him why he wanted to see Ms. Jones and he showed her the envelope which contained the letter. She took the envelope from him and went into the back office. Before leaving she asked him to have a seat in a waiting area. After several minutes, she returned and asked him to come with her to meet Ms. Jones. Ms. Jones introduced herself and said that she had read the letter and understood that he was seeking to get a job with AT&T. She proceeded to administer a test to him. He completed the test which consisted of basic mathematics and English questions. He was comfortable that he had done well. He knew that he was not good at mathematics, but he felt that he had done well enough to pass the test. She had the test scored and he did indeed pass and directed him to fill out an applicant form.

He filled out the application without much difficulty but left one of the questions blank. This particular question asked for his draft classification.

He was called back into the office of Ms. Jones and she looked over the application form and noticed that the question regarding his draft classification had been left blank. When she asked him about the question left blank, he told her that he did not know what the question meant. His response was not true. He did indeed know what the question meant. He knew that if he had registered for the draft as he was required to do, he could be sent to Vietnam to fight in a war. He had heard that several young men from Santa Maria who had entered the United States on a visitor's visa and had voluntarily joined the army and had been sent to Vietnam. In the process they received their green cards and were allowed to remain legally in the United States. Unfortunately, not all of them returned, some were killed in combat. She told him that he had passed the test and that he would be hired to work for AT&T but he had to have a draft classification. She explained that he was required to go to any of the offices of the Selective Service to register for the draft and that he would be given a classification on a card which had to be brought to her before his hiring could be finalized.

This was an obstacle which he had not anticipated but he wanted a job so he knew that this was something that he could not avoid. He pretended that he was not aware of what Ms. Jones was saying about his requirement to register for the draft after he had turned 18. The year was 1970 and the Vietnam War was going on and he was not particularly excited about the prospect of being drafted into the United States Army and being sent to Vietnam to fight in a war he did not know much about.

There was no way to get around it and he went to the Selective Service office he had seen on 42nd Street and registered for the draft. He was given a Selective Service registration card and on it he saw that he was classified as 1A, the designation which gave him the highest ranking as someone who could be drafted into the United States Army at any time.

He was not happy about this development, but he accepted it with a bit of fatalism. He needed and wanted a job and he had no choice. Four months ago, he was a high school student in Santa Maria and now he was registered for the draft and faced the reality that he could, at any time, be drafted into the United States Army and sent to fight a war in Vietnam.

He had been familiar with the situation of Muhammad Ali's refusal to be conscripted into the United States Army. He was also familiar with what was reported as the words of Ali when he said, "I ain't got no argument with no Viet Cong. If I have to fight for freedom, I will fight for freedom right here in America."

He went on to ask the question,

"Why should I fight for freedom in Vietnam when my people here are not free right here in America."

At the time the jury was out on whether or not Ali was doing the right thing by refusing to be drafted. There were many others who also refused but mostly they took a different route. Some simply packed their bags and went north to Canada, while others burned their draft cards in public and dared the authorities to find and arrest them.

He had become a fan of Muhammad Ali when he defeated Sonny Liston in 1964 to win the heavy weight championship of the world.

On the day that he registered for the draft, he remembered his childhood friend who was serving in the United States Army in Vietnam. His friend had migrated to Brooklyn, New York in the summer of 1964. There he finished junior high school and went on to high school. After two years of high school, he was bored and fell in with other teenagers who were not going in the right direction. He decided that he would get out of Brooklyn and the way he decided to do that was by joining the United States Army. He dropped out of high school and joined the army at the age of seventeen. After basic training at Fort Dix in New Jersey, he was sent to Vietnam in 1968. He was now back from the war, but he was not the same person. His experience had had a profound effect on him. Terrence had asked him about his experience in Vietnam. He was honest and said,

"For the first six months after I arrived in Vietnam, I burned human shit."

Terrence was puzzled and his friend saw the puzzled look on his face and further explained,

"Yes, I burned human shit every day, that was my job."

Terrence nodded his head, and his friend went on to tell him that he saw many soldiers on both sides get killed.

"War is hell," was the description of the Vietnam War that his friend gave. These were the thoughts which came to Terrence's mind on the day that he registered for the draft. He thought of his childhood friend burning the shit of his fellow soldiers and he thought of the prospect of having to kill other human beings or being killed himself.

He was designated as 1A for the draft. This meant that he would be able to be hired for this reputable company, which at the time was the not only the largest and most successful company in the United States but the world. It also meant that he could be drafted at any time. If drafted, he had three options. He could report for induction or he could ignore the draft notification which would mean that he was committing a crime for which he could be arrested and imprisoned. Lastly, if drafted, he could return to Santa Maria. This would mean that he would be giving up the opportunity to live and work in the United States. He knew that he really only had one option, if drafted, he would report to be inducted.

Later, he learned of another option. This option was the military draft lottery. This option was purely based on 'the luck of the draw'. The Selective Service had instituted the lottery system as a component of the draft. They could not accommodate all the males who were of military age, so the draft lottery was instituted. The 365 days of the year were placed in a 'hat' and the order that the birthdates were pulled out would be the order for the draft. If your birthdate was drawn first, then you would be sure to be drafted. The general expectation was that you could be drafted if your birthday fell between 1 and 200. Terrence's lottery number was 302. This left him relatively assured that he would not be drafted. Lady luck had been kind to him. In the summer of 1971, he received his new classification in the mail and the 1A classification had been changed to 1H. He no longer had to worry about being drafted into the army and being sent to fight a war in Vietnam for a cause he did not fully understand in a country which he did not know the location on a map of the world.

During the time of uncertainty about the draft, he thought of another friend from his neighborhood in Santa Maria. His friend's name was Bert and he had moved into the neighborhood three years before Terrence left to live in Harlem. Bert became quite popular because he was a talker and a dreamer. His big dream was to go to the United States to join the army. He was fascinated by persons in military uniforms and by persons in uniforms in general. Each day he told the other neighborhood boys that he would go to the United States to join the army and that he was looking forward to going to Vietnam to fight in the war. He never said that he knew what the war was about. He had only heard of the war and heard that the United States was involved because they were fighting on the side of South Vietnam against North Vietnam.

Bert's desire to join the U.S. Army was all consuming to him. He said that he researched how he could join. He said that he would go to Puerto Rico, which was a territory of the United States and he would enlist there. At one point, he told everyone that he was leaving in a week and that all the arrangements had been made. He said that he would be met at the airport in Puerto Rico by representatives of the U.S. Army and they had arranged for his entry into Puerto Rico with the immigration authorities.

On the day that he left Santa Maria, he was scheduled on the 8:00am flight to Puerto Rico. Several of his friends gathered at his home early in the morning and wished him well. His parents were apprehensive, but he assured them that he knew what he was doing and that everything had been arranged. He said the representatives of the U.S. Army were expecting him and they were happy to have him. Some of the boys who went to his house that morning to say goodbye were a bit jealous. He was getting all the attention and very soon he would be in the U.S. Army.

The taxi which would take him to airport arrived at 6:45am. He walked down the steps to the taxi accompanied by his parents, siblings and friends. He hugged and kissed everyone and said goodbye before entering the taxi. He was obviously cherishing the moment and he said his goodbyes and left. Terrence wondered if he had any second thoughts regarding going to join the U. S. Army.

After he entered the back seat of the taxi and closed the door. He sat on the left side opposite the driver who sat on the right because the steering wheel of the car was on the right side. As the taxi headed east, he looked backward and waved until the taxi was out of sight.

Later that day, at 5:10pm, as the neighborhood boys were playing cricket in the park in front of the house where Bert and his family lived, a taxi came down the street and stopped in front of his house. Bert got out of the taxi with the small suitcase that he had left with that morning, and without saying anything to his friends, he entered his house and closed the door behind him.

His friends stopped playing and ran over to his house and knocked on the front door. They wanted to know what had happened that caused him to return on the same day that he left to join the U.S. Army. Their knocks on the front door were unanswered. They went back to the playing field and resumed playing cricket.

He was not seen for another week. When he finally emerged from his house, he told a story that there was a mix-up and that he would return to Puerto Rico shortly to join the army. Up to a year later when Terrence had left to live permanently in the United States, Bert had not yet resolved the mix-up and he was still in Santa Maria.

Two years after Terrence moved to Harlem, he learned that Bert had managed to get to New York City and was living in the Bronx. Shortly after moving to New York City, Bert met a friend from Santa Maria in Maurice's Barbershop and told him that he was now a medical doctor at Harlem Hospital on Lennox Avenue. During their meeting at the barbershop, Bert was wearing medical scrubs and had a stethoscope around his neck. It was difficult to conceptualize that Bert had become a doctor in such a short period of time when, in fact, he had not completed high school and he had not attended university. Bert was not a doctor as he had told the person who saw him dressed in hospital scrubs with a stethoscope around his neck.

As a young boy, in all likelihood, his quick actions saved the life of his younger brother when he had a terrible accident. Their family lived directly in front of the park where all the boys from the village played cricket and football. It was on the front steps of their house that one boy almost killed another boy who batted and did not field, by hitting him with a cricket bat on the side of his head. In the case of Bert and his younger brother, his quick actions likely saved his brother's life when he was impaled on the metal handle of a shopping cart.

It was a normal summer day and the neighborhood youngsters were enjoying their summer break. During the summer months, young boys of the neighborhood gathered in the park to play cricket or football. Others, at times, came to the park just to hang out and talk with their friends. Bert's younger brother did not play cricket or football with the older boys who were his brother's age, but he did find ways of getting into his fair share of mischief.

On this particular day, several boys were seated on the steps of Bert's house and Terrence and Bert's young brother were on the gallery along with two others, a girl and a boy. The girl was hearing impaired and had difficulty enunciating her words correctly because of her impairment. She was often teased and bullied by persons outside of the village. At times, she was teased by the kids who hung around the park as well. She was not teased because of her impairment by her friends. She was teased because she was from the village and all the kids in the village were at one time or other teased by their peers. No one escaped the teasing. It was something that each was resigned to when it happened.

On this day, one of the boy's had been sent by his parents to purchase items from the market and he was sent with a shopping cart which had four wheels and a single curved metal handle. The cart could have been pushed or pulled by using this handle. The boy with the shopping cart, upon returning from the market which was located just down the street from the park, stopped to play cricket before he returned home where his mother was waiting for the goods which she had sent him to buy. He gave no consideration to the fact that his mother was waiting for the items to cook the family dinner. He placed the shopping cart with the curved single handle in the yard of Bert's house right next to the gallery. He could have placed it on the gallery or on the steps and all would have been well. The fact that he placed the cart in the yard next to the gallery turned out to be an incredible stroke of misfortune for Bert's younger brother.

The gallery was about four feet off the ground. Bert's younger brother and the girl with the hearing impairment were teasing each other. At one point, Bert's younger brother hit her and ran, as she ran after him, he climbed over the gallery and jumped backwards to the ground. Unfortunately, that is where the cart with the single curved metal handle had been placed and he jumped backwards onto it. After he jumped, there was a piercing loud scream, and everyone looked in his direction. He was standing on his tippy toes and the metal handle of the cart was in his rectum. Bert had been sitting on the steps of the house and when he saw what had happened, he ran to his brother to help him and quickly extricated his brother from the handle of the cart. His brother was now bleeding profusely, and he picked him up and took him inside the house. The ambulance was immediately called, and it arrived and took him to the hospital where he had surgery to repair the damage to his intestines. Bert's younger brother remained in the hospital for a period of two months. It was determined that his intestines had been ruptured and the bacteria had seriously contaminated his stomach, which in turn could have killed him.

Maurice's Barbershop was a regular spot where Santa Marians met. It was located on 125th Street just off Madison Avenue. It was literally around the corner from the cleaners owned by Terrence's father. Maurice, the owner of the barbershop, was also from Santa Maria. Maurice was considered to be a very good barber, but he had a number of peculiarities that were difficult to fathom. It was always best to be the first to arrive at the barbershop if you wanted to get a haircut without having to wait for an interminably long period of time. He was the only barber in the shop and he refused to hire other barbers or rent the additional chairs to other barbers. He took at least an hour to cut each person's hair. He was meticulous and you could never tell him to hurry up, that would be disconcerting to him and he would go more slowly. If you tried to tell him how you wanted your hair to be cut, he would get visibly upset and say that you should not tell him how to do his job. He often said that he was the expert, and he did not want to be told what to do.

The tailor who had taken over the cleaners after the death of Terrence's father went to get a haircut from Maurice. When he sat in the chair, he started to tell Maurice how he wanted his hair to be cut. Maurice interrupted him and said,

"You are a tailor, right? I have brought things to you to be repaired and I did not tell you how to do your sewing. I am the barber, do not tell me how to cut your hair."

The tailor allowed Maurice to cut his hair on that occasion, but he found another barber. He never went back to Maurice for a haircut and Maurice said it was the tailor's loss, not his.

Maurice was a middle-aged man who lived in the Bronx with a girlfriend who was half his age. He was possessive and did not allow her to be out of his sight. She accompanied him to his barbershop every day. While in the barbershop, she was required to sweep and mop the floor. This, she was required to do several times during the course of the day. Additionally, she was not permitted to speak with any of the male customers who were there for a haircut. Then one day, she disappeared. The rumor was that on a busy Saturday, she took a broom and was sweeping in front of the barber shop by the entrance and when Maurice was busy cutting the hair of a customer, she simply walked away with only the clothes on her back. He had managed to intimidate her to the point of being deathly afraid of him. He owned a gun and had previously threatened to use it if she tried to leave him.

Maurice lived in the Bronx and made the journey to Harlem every day for work. Not surprisingly, he did not get along with his neighbors. During the summer months, the teenagers who lived in the apartment building where he did, often gathered in the front of the building just to chat. Maurice did not like the fact that they stood there and accused them of loitering. His comments to them were disparaging and he went so far as to tell them that they were lazy and worthless thieves. He accused them of being the ones who had carried out two recent break-ins in the building. He reminded them of where he lived in the apartment building and told them to stay away from his apartment, otherwise he would shoot anyone who dared to break-in to his apartment.

One day he returned home from work and found his apartment completely empty. All the contents had been stolen including all of his clothes and furniture. He called the police who came to investigate. He told the police that he suspected that the teenage boys who often gathered in the front of the building were responsible for the theft. He also told the police that he had a gun and that he would have shot them if he had come home and found them in the act. The police asked him to show the gun to them and he did. He was promptly arrested for having an unlicensed firearm. He was subsequently evicted from his apartment for making threats to his young neighbors. His next-door neighbor told him that when the robbery occurred, he had seen the men removing his belongings, but he thought that he was moving because the men came in a professional moving van. It was never determined who was responsible for the robbery. Other neighbors speculated that it was his former girlfriend who arranged it. She was never questioned because he was unable to give the police any details of her current whereabouts. Others speculated that the culprits were likely the young boys that often gathered in front of his building. The ones he had disparaged by calling them worthless thieves.

When Terrence heard of the misfortune which had befallen Maurice, he was not at all surprised and he also felt no empathy toward him. Terrence had been a regular customer at Maurice's Barbershop and had put up with his nonsensical behavior because he was a good barber.

Maurice's behavior contributed to Terrence's childhood friend, Tess, being thirty minutes late for his own wedding. Terrence and Tess had been friends since their childhood days in Santa Maria. They had lived on the same street and often spent time together along with Tess's younger brother.

Tess knew that Maurice was a good barber and decided to get a haircut on the morning of his wedding. Terrence had been asked by Tess to be the best man at his wedding and Terrence agreed. Because Tess was scheduled to get a haircut, Terrence decided that he would have Maurice cut his hair as well. They both wanted to look sharp for the wedding.

Getting haircuts under normal circumstance was pretty innocuous on the surface but they were a bit apprehensive because they both knew that that Maurice took over an hour to cut each person's hair. To add to that, Maurice's barbershop was located in Harlem and the church where the wedding ceremony would take place was located in the East Flatbush in Brooklyn. Both of them made appointments for 9:00am and 10:00am respectively. They arrived promptly at 8:55am with the expectation that one of them would immediately get the chance to get started. Upon their arrival another customer was already sitting in Maurice's chair getting a haircut. Maurice assured them that he would be finished in a few minutes. The few minutes that he promised was reality thirty minutes because he did not finish with the other customer until 9:30 am. Terrence thought that this could be a problem and suggested to Tess that perhaps they should forego the haircuts in the interest of time. They both knew that Maurice was meticulous in his craft and would not take kindly to them telling him that they were in a hurry and that he needed to speed up. Tess made the judgement to wait to get the haircuts from Maurice because his wedding ceremony was scheduled for 3:30pm. Tess was first and his haircut lasted for one hour and ten minutes. It started at 9:35am and ended at 10:45am. Once again, Terrence suggested that they should leave and head back to Brooklyn. Tess said that it was okay and told him to proceed with his haircut and that they had enough time.

When Terrence sat in the chair, he reminded Maurice that Tess was getting married at 3:30pm and that they had to hurry up to get back to Brooklyn. Maurice sternly responded that for him to do a good job he could not rush. He further said that he had a reputation to uphold, and he could not do a bad job because other Santa Marians would be attending the wedding, so he had to make sure to do his best. Sure enough, he took his time. Once again, he took an hour and ten minutes to complete Terrence's haircut. He started at 10:45am and ended at 11:55am. They left the barbershop at noon thinking that they had enough time to drive to East Flatbush in Brooklyn, shower without messing up their hair, get dressed and arrive at the church at approximately 3:00pm for the ceremony at 3:30pm.

They immediately got into Tess's car and drove east on 125th Street to the Eastside highway. As they drove, Terrence thought of the barbershops in Santa Maria and realized that the barbers there acted somewhat like Maurice. As a small boy of nine or ten, going to the barbershop for a haircut was never fun, it was more like torture. The three prominent barbers in the city at the time were Goody, Roy and Cooper. The proprietor of Goody Barbershop was a man with the last name Goodwin. Many people went to his barbershop but the young boys who went there or more correctly the young boys who were sent there by their parents or guardians were treated quite differently to the boys who went with their parents. If you went alone, you had to wait until all the adults had been attended to. Once you got into the chair to get your haircut, Goody would cut your hair the way he saw fit, it did not matter what you told him he did it the way he wanted to. Once while cutting Terrence's hair, he made fun of him and said that his head had scars as if he had been in World War 2. He had a scar in his head as a result of a fall he had on the metal frame of a bed in the house. He was playing with his sister when he was four or five and fell backwards onto a metal post and cut the back of his head. His head bled profusely. Now a few years later he was embarrassed when Goody made fun of him after seeing the scar. In addition to having to wait for interminably long periods of time when you wanted to get a haircut, Goody, at times, played pranks on the young boys. A typical prank would be for Goody to send you on an errand. He would tell you to go to the home of one of his friends to pick up an item and bring back to his barbershop. He would say,

"Do you know my friend Boots who lives at the top of Rodney Street?"

Most people in the community knew Boots because he was quite a popular character. The boy being sent on the errand usually knew and answered in the affirmative. Goody would then say,

"Go to Boots and tell him that I sent you for the wood stretcher."

Not knowing that there was no such thing as a wood stretcher, as a young boy, you would be on your way. Upon your arrival at the house where Boots lived, you would knock on the door and when Boots answered, you would announce that Goody sent you for the wood stretcher. Boots would then say that he would be right back. He would close his front door and leave you to wait outside of his home.

A few minutes later, he would open the door and give you a large box which was very heavy. The contents of the box could not be seen because it was taped shut. Boots would then say to be careful with the very heavy box and told you to be sure not to drop the box under any circumstances because you would damage what was inside. As a small boy you would lift the heavy box and struggle with it making sure that it was not dropped and arrive back at the barbershop and deliver it to Goody. He would then direct you to put it in a back room of the barbershop with the pile of other boxes. The prank was then complete and you had to continue to wait for your haircut. It was only later that you would find out that there was no such thing as a wood stretcher because obviously wood could not be stretched. One young boy, after receiving the heavy box from Boots, decided to open the box on his way back to the barbershop and saw that several clay bricks and pieces of metal were in the box. He realized that Goody and Boots were having fun at his expense and decided to get even with Goody. On his way back to the barbershop he stopped in the Methodist church yard and 'took a shit' in the box and resealed it with the tape and took it back to Goody who directed him to put it in the back room on the floor with the other boxes.

Goody must have found out what this boy had done because after that incident he stopped sending the neighborhood boys to get the wood stretcher.

Another barber in Ovals was called Cooper and none of the boys liked going to him because he did not have electric tools and it was physically painful to get a haircut. He used manual clippers and scissors to give haircuts. If you received a haircut from Cooper, you were laughed at by your friends and family members because he would leave big patches in your head and the haircut looked like it had been done by your mother or a sister. Cooper was notorious for spitting while giving someone a haircut. It appeared that he had a perpetual cold, and he would cough and unceremoniously spit over your head into the street. His barbershop was actually the living room of his house which was built very close to the street. The house was no more than three feet from the sidewalk.

A third barbershop opened in the city and the proprietor was a tall man named Roy. He employed several barbers and he had a very good clientele. Most of the customers were from their late teens to their early forties.

Terrence and his friends stopped going to Cooper and Goody and became clients at Roy's Barbershop. Here they did not have to worry about any of the barbers spitting over their heads into the street but more importantly their tools were electric and they did not have to suffer the indignity of having big gaps in their hair at the completion of their haircuts. Two of the barbers employed by Roy were Leroy and Ted. Terrence preferred to have his haircuts from Leroy. One day Terrence asked Leroy to give him a shorter haircut than usual and Leroy asked if he was sure that he wanted a shorter haircut and he said yes. Leroy then took his electric clippers and cut a line in his head starting from the front all the way to the back of his head. Terrence jumped from the chair and said to Leroy,

"What are you doing?"

In response, Leroy said laughing,

"You asked for a shorter haircut, so I am giving you what you asked for."

Terrence was upset and responded,

"I asked for a shorter haircut, but you know I did not mean this short."

Leroy continued to laugh, and Terrence knew that there was nothing that could be done to salvage a bad situation. He was bald in the middle of his head. It was tantamount to having a reverse mohawk. He sat back in the chair and asked Leroy to fix it as best as he could, and Leroy proceeded to shave the rest of his hair to make it even. As a result, he ended up with a bald head. As he left the barbershop Terrence was in agony. How could he go home with a bald head? What would his friends say when they saw him? How would a thirteen-year-old go to school with a bald head and not be laughed at? His agony made him go directly to the store where he bought a straw hat. He would wear this straw hat every day until his hair grew back. Of course, the straw hat did not prevent him from being teased by his family members, his friends in the village, his classmates at school and even his teachers. He could not wear the hat in class, so everyone saw his bald head. One of his teachers resorted to calling him 'baldy'. His friends in the village simply snatched his hat off the first time they saw him wearing it. When they asked what happened to him, he told the truth and told them that Leroy did it. They laughed and made sure that they would never tell Leroy to give them a shorter haircut. Terrence and his friends used Ted as their barber from then on.

Tess and Terrence entered the eastside highway at 125th street and headed south to lower Manhattan where they would take the Brooklyn Bridge over to Brooklyn. Unfortunately, when they got to 96th street, they ran into a major traffic jam which was caused by an accident. This traffic jam caused them to be delayed by an hour. Saturday was always a busy time on the highway and the accident made the situation worse. Tess and Terrence were now panicking wondering if they would make it on time to the church. After they got beyond the accident, they were able to get downtown and get on the Brooklyn Bridge when they ran into another traffic jam because of another accident and another delay of an hour. Now they were certain that they would not make it to the church on time. Terrence felt guilty, because as the best man it was his responsibility to ensure that they arrived on time and also it was he who initially made the suggestion to go to Maurice on the morning of the wedding.

They arrived at the house where they would get dressed at approximately 3:10 pm. It was impossible for them to get to church for the wedding to begin at 3:30pm. They showered and got dressed as quickly as they could and left the house at 3:30pm and headed to the church. This time Terrence drove and Tess sat in the front passenger seat. Tess was nervous for being late and he was also nervous because he was getting married. To get to the church, they had to drive on Church Avenue which was always very busy on Saturdays. Church Avenue was located in a commercial district in East Flatbush where many people from the Caribbean lived and where there were many 'mom and pop' stores which sold cheap Chinese made merchandise. They arrived at the church at 4:00pm, a full thirty minutes late.

When they arrived, the bride was in the vestry with her aunt that she lived with and they were both crying. The minister who would be conducting the marriage ceremony was upset that his schedule for the day was now in jeopardy and he told them that he had another wedding scheduled for 4:30pm. Some of the wedding guests were milling around on the steps of the church awaiting the arrival of the groom and best man and wondering if the groom had changed his mind.

Tess went into the vestry and apologized to his bride to be and her aunt. The minister then escorted Terrence and Tess to the altar and positioned them in their places. Her aunt then helped her to fix her make-up which had been smeared from the tears. After her make-up was fixed, the bride and her bridesmaids went to the entrance of the church and the organist started to play, 'Here Comes the Bride'. She walked up the aisle with her bridesmaids in tow and the ceremony began.

There were no more hitches and the minister hurried through the wedding ceremony and it was completed in thirty minutes. It appeared that everyone was happy. As the wedding party exited the church, the bride, groom and guests for the next wedding were waiting outside. Tess was especially happy because he had found a bride and the bride was happy that she had found a husband.

Terrence and Tess were childhood friends and they were the same age. Tess had a younger brother who always wanted to tag along when Tess and Terrence wanted to go to the beach or movies by themselves. One Saturday morning the three of them decided to cut open a honeybee hive to extract the honey. They had never done this before, but they thought that it could not have been too difficult. The honeybee hive was just up the hill from where they lived. Tess said that he would be the one to cut the hive and extract the honey. The honeybees had made their hive in a big hole in a concrete wall. In order to cut the hive to get the honey, Tess would have put his hand into the hole. He got dressed in an old jacket which belonged to his grandfather and put on woolen gloves to cover his hands. He then used an old tee shirt to cover his head and neck and cut out holes for his eyes. He then placed a cap on his head. He thought that he had covered all areas of his body to prevent the bees from stinging him. They then walked up the hill to get the honey. With Terrence and Tess's little brother standing a good distance away, Tess proceeded to put his hand in the hole where the honeybee hive was located. In a short time, Tess screamed and pulled his hand from the hole and started running back down the hill with a swarm of honeybees all around him. Terrence and Tess's younger brother, from a distance, laughed so hard that they fell on the ground. While Tess was running with the swarm of bees all around him, he was attempting to swat them away from his head and also attempting to take off the old jacket that he was wearing. The honeybees had gone up the sleeve of the jacket and were stinging him. That was the first and only time that they sought to cut a honeybee hive to get honey.

Tess arrived in New York City one year after Terrence did. Tess came on a visitor's visa in 1971 under the auspices of his aunt who was an American citizen. He had no intention of returning to Santa Maria after the expiration of his visitor's visa. Initially, he lived with his aunt, but he quickly found a job at Daitch Shopwell supermarket which was only two blocks away from where he lived. This was the same supermarket where Terrence would first see Luz Fernandez.

Tess's future wife also worked at the supermarket. She lived with her aunt in Brooklyn which was quite a distance away. She was from Guyana, the only English-speaking country in South America. She had also come to the United States on a visitor's visa under the auspices of her aunt. She also had no intention of leaving the United States after the expiration of her visitor's visa.

It was known by young male immigrants from the Caribbean that the surest way to acquire a green card to live permanently in the United States was to enlist in the U.S. Army and be sent to Vietnam or to marry an American citizen. And how did young men, who were seeking to get married to get a permanent visa, know if the young lady they were marrying was an American citizen? If she was born in the United States, she was indeed an American citizen by birth. So the simple way to find out was to just ask her where she was born. The question was innocuous, and it did not have to be revealed that there was a great reason for the question. It was also possible to acquire a green card if an immigrant with a green card married another immigrant who did not have one.

In the case of Tess and his new bride, both assumed that the other had already acquired a green card and that each was residing legally in the United States.

After they had been married for about three months, Tess decided that he would delicately approach his new wife with the subject of her sponsoring him to get his green card. Of course, she was surprised because she too was considering approaching him about sponsoring her. Tess was shocked when she revealed that she did not have a green card and that she was hoping that he would sponsor her.

The house that Bert lived in was directly in front of the playing field in the neighborhood. Before Bert's family moved in, the house was occupied by the oldest lady in the community. It is said that she lived to be 100. She lived alone but would be visited three times per day by her son to bring her meals. She had the reputation of being eccentric because she never left the house but would come out onto her porch for the sole reason of emptying her night soil over the gallery. It was not unusual to see her come out on her gallery with a utensil containing urine and tossing it over the side of the railing.

After she passed away and before Bert's family moved in, the steps of the house became a gathering place for the neighborhood boys. For anyone who grew up in this neighborhood during the late sixties, this house will be remembered as the place where one boy almost killed another boy over a dispute while they were playing cricket.

During the summer months, the neighborhood boys played cricket in the park from shortly after sunrise until sunset. Sunday was the day of worship and many of the boys were required by their parents to attend mass and also Sunday school offered by their church. Some parents restricted their sons from playing cricket on Sundays. Those who were restricted often managed to circumvent the restrictions and played anyway. They were willing to take the chance and suffer the consequences if caught.

One weekday afternoon, cricket was being played as was the norm. What was not the norm was that one of the players decided that he did not want to field after his team had batted.

There is a cardinal rule in neighborhood cricket that after you batted you must field when it was your turn to do so. The only circumstance which would allow you not to field after you batted, was if you had been called home by your parents or guardians. On this fateful day, one boy decided that he would not field. He had batted and had scored a few runs before getting out. After batting he refused to field. He sat on the steps of this house where the old lady had lived and laughed when he was told by a player on the opposing team that he was required to be on the field. The player who admonished him and asked him to be on the field was now batting. Once again, this boy was asked to go onto the field and once again, he refused and laughed about his refusal. To everyone's dismay, the batter went over to the steps of the house and hit him directly to the side of his head with the cricket bat. The assault was so swift, that no one had the opportunity to intercede to stop the boy who carried it out. A cricket bat is flat with pronounced edges. The assailant turned the bat sideways and delivered the blow directly to the side of the head of the boy who had refused to field. After the blow was delivered, the victim's eyes looked glazed, and he fell unconscious to the ground.

Everyone was in shock regarding what had happened right before their eyes. In the past, it was not unusual for the boys to fight each other. They fought with their fists and the most one would expect was to get a black eye or a bruise and in a short space of time, they would be friends again. Neighborhood boys did not fight each other with weapons, weapons were only used if the fight was with someone from outside of the neighborhood.

The victim was picked up by the other boys and put to lay flat on the cricket field. This had to be done because when he fell on the steps, where he was sitting when he received the blow to his temple, he fell like a ton of bricks and his body was all crumpled up.

Seeing the severity of the situation, one of the boys ran home and told his parents who called the ambulance. The police were also called. The ambulance arrived about forty-five minutes later and took the still unconscious boy to the hospital.

The police arrived after the ambulance had left and they were told what had happened. The assailant had already left the scene and was nowhere to be found. The police were told where he lived, and they went to his home, but he was not there. He was not found for several weeks. He had left his neighborhood home and was staying with relatives in the countryside.

The victim remained in the hospital for three months and it was rumored that he had suffered brain damage. Whether or not he suffered brain damage was never substantiated. What was substantiated was that he never returned to the neighborhood park to play cricket or to participate in any neighborhood activity.

This entire fiasco had a sobering effect on the neighborhood boys. They almost witnessed the death of a friend right before their eyes. In the years that followed, no other boy batted during a cricket match and refused to field when he was required to do so.

It was with these thoughts of his old neighborhood in Santa Maria in his mind that Terrence left the Selective Service office where he had registered for the draft.

Armed with verification that he had registered for the draft, he returned to see Ms. Jones at the headquarters of AT&T. He was delighted to be informed by her that he had successfully met the requirements to be hired by the company and he was directed to return on the following Monday to begin his orientation.

◊◊

Chapter 5

The decision not to return to their father's house was made by the two older sisters. They had had enough of the abuse meted out by their father. Each weekend was horrific and it seemed to get worse each time. To suffer abuse at the hands of your father who should be there to protect you was unimaginable. The children kept hoping that things would get better but instead they seemed to get worse. The psychological damage being done to all six children was immeasurable, especially to Terrence who was yet to reach his ninth birthday.

It was 1961 and all six of the siblings were essentially homeless. The older siblings had decided not to return to their father's house and the others went along with their decision, now it was up to their aunt, their mother's sister to decide if they could live with her and her family. Fortunately, their aunt accepted them and thus the move became permanent, and they did not return to their father's house.

At the time, Terrence did not understand the gravity of the situation. One day he overheard his aunt telling one of his grandmother's sisters that her sister, our mother Ruby, had come to her in a dream and told her not to allow her six children to return to their father's house because they were being abused and it was only getting worse each time it happened. Thus, she felt that it was her obligation to abide by the wishes of her deceased sister even though she knew that the task would be difficult. Their aunt's home was always their refuge as they sought to escape the wrath of their father each weekend when he was in a drunken stupor.

Their aunt's house was in walking distance from their father's house and was located in an area on the outskirts of the city called Ovals. Officially, Ovals was an area of five blocks and was bordered by Drake Street on the south and Rodney Street on the north. On the east was East Street, and on the west, it was bordered by Market Street.

It was a relatively small area, on the south side of the capital city. To many residents of Santa Maria, the boundaries of Ovals were never definitively clear. On the south side, the line of demarcation between Ovals and Michael's Village was Drake Street, however, the boys who lived in Michael's Village were also considered to be residents of Ovals. The same thing was true on the north side where the line of demarcation between Ovals and the city was Rodney Street, however, it was extended several streets over to Tanner Street, which was four short blocks to the north.

Terrence and his sisters and brother moved to live with their aunt and her family in 1961. Their aunt's family had seven persons, five children and their aunt and her husband. Now there was an increase by six to bring the total to thirteen persons living in a relatively small three-bedroom house.

At the time, Ovals was considered as a lower middle-class area. Several civil servants lived in Ovals. Civil servants were medium ranking individuals who worked for government departments such as the police force, the post office and customs.

The house was on Temple and Nelson Streets. Temple Street ran south to north and lead right to the Anglican cathedral. The Anglican cathedral was a short five-minute walk away. Directly across the street in front of the house was the Ovals playing field which had produced many of the island's top sportsmen. It was here that Terrence spent many of his waking hours when he was not in school or involved with school activities. It was actually here that many of the boys in Ovals spent their time after school and especially on Saturdays and to a lesser extent on Sundays. The summer holidays were all spent in this playing field. It was here that many lifelong friendships were formed.

On the northwest corner of Temple and Nelson Streets was a wholesale business owned by a local man named Johnathan Jones. His father was named Isaac Jones who apparently started the business as a local shop and his oldest son, Johnathan, had managed to transform it to be largest wholesale business on the island of Santa Maria. Johnathan Jones had grown his business to the point where he became so successful that he was considered to be the richest man on the island. It was rumored that when the government could not meet its payroll, Johnathan Jones lent the government the money to pay the workers. His main source of income was the wholesale importation and distribution of Heineken beer.

Jonathan Jones had two brothers, one was named Alvin who was a preacher in a Pentecostal Church and another named John who had the nickname, Executioner. It is said that he got that nickname because as a young boy, he would catch lizards and cut them open and afterwards use a needle and thread from his mother to sew them back up before setting them free. Terrence knew on a first-hand basis that he also tortured little boys who did not know how to swim. As a little boy of about 8 or 9 Terrence had gone to Fort James, with family members. Fort James was a very popular beach. Executioner had offered to take the young boys on the beach for a ride on his boat. Executioner lived in Ovals and everyone knew him. He did indeed take them for a short ride, but he did not bring them all the way back to the shallow waters where he picked them up. He stayed a short distance offshore and told everyone that they had to swim back to the shore. Executioner knew that there were some boys on his boat, who did not know how to swim. He simply picked up the hesitant ones, including Terrence and threw them overboard into the sea and told them to swim to the shore. The boys who could not swim learned how to swim that day. To Executioner's credit, he kept a watchful eye and ensured that all the boys made it safely to the shore.

To the boys, that could not swim, it would have been traumatic to be tossed into the sea and to literally sink or swim. To Executioner and the others, it was a way to have some fun and have the boys learn how to swim without the formality of taking swimming lessons or being taught by a trusted relative or family friend.

Alvin was a preacher and was not at all like his brother, Executioner. Alvin also owned a small shop on the corner of Temple and Rodney Streets directly behind his brother's wholesale business on the corner of Temple and Nelson Streets. It was in this small retail shop that Terrence met another boy who would become his closest childhood friend. This boy lived three houses to the east of the shop and despite the fact that he was only nine years old, he worked in Alvin's retail shop selling behind the counter and carefully wrapping flour, rice and sugar into one-pound paper bags. Alvin would buy flower, sugar and rice in 50lb bags from his brother, Jonathan and then his workers would have to parcel out these 50lb bags into smaller 1lb paper bags for retail sales. One day Terrence was sent to Alvin's retail shop to buy a pound of sugar and there he met Trevor who sold him the sugar. Trevor parceled out the pound of sugar and it was meticulously wrapped. Terrence watched as Trevor scooped out a portion of sugar and placed some from the scoop into the brown paper bag that he had opened and placed on a scale. The scale had to be perfectly balanced thus ensuring that the right amount of sugar had been placed in the bag. On the ceiling of Alvin's retail shop, he had two framed scriptures. The first one said,

"What shall it profit a man if he gained the whole world and lose his soul?"

The second one said,

"It is easier for a camel to pass through the eye of a needle than for a rich man to enter the kingdom of heaven."

Alvin was a businessman but, apparently, he did not want to be rich like his brother who owned the wholesale business importing and distributing Heineken beer. He also did not want to be like his younger brother who tortured lizards and little boys who had not yet learned to swim. He eventually closed his shop and became a full-fledged pastor in the Pentecostal Church. Terrence was not sure if he closed the retail shop because it was failing, or he did not want to become rich.

Terrence and Trevor became close friends and their friendship continued through high school and beyond. Trevor managed to secure a position with one of the airlines after graduation, so he was able to travel extensively throughout the Caribbean and particularly to New York where some of his family members lived.

The Jones family also consisted of several beautiful sisters. One, named Janice, worked in the retail shop with her brother Alvin when she was a young girl. An older one worked, named Gloria worked in the wholesale business.

Jonathan, the successful owner of the wholesale business was an ardent cricket fan and played cricket with the boys in the park from time to time. He did not really play in the true sense, but he often batted and gave any player who was able to get him out fifty cents to purchase a Heineken malt from the bar on the corner of Hawkins Street and Temple Street. The bar was owned by a Dominican family and it was run by the son, named Alfred. Johnathan was also the importer of the malt that was purchased for the boys when they got him out. At times, he would give the player who got him out a single dollar bill. He was a good batsman and it was difficult to get him out. No one knew if he was also a good bowler and fielder because he never did these two things, his playing involved only batting and giving malts or dollar bills to the young cricketers.

Johnathan had apparently inherited the business from his father and he expanded it and developed it to become the successful wholesale business. It was rumored that his father was an obeah man who had made a pact with the devil. No one established if this rumor was true or not. All it took for a rumor like this to start was for some jealous person to make the statement and it would be repeated over and over until it became folklore.

The mother of the Jones clan lived at the bottom of Rodney Street with her daughters. The three sons were all married and lived on their own. Mrs. Jones was a short woman who was often seen walking around the neighborhood. From time to time, she stopped and chatted with her neighbors and with friends that she met while she walked around. One afternoon as Terrence was standing on the corner where he lived, Mrs. Jones walked by and stopped to chat with him. She told him that she was from Liberta, the same village where his father was born and that she knew his father. She also went on to tell Terrence that she was related to his father and that consequently that meant that she was also related to him. He did not know how to respond and nodded his head and she continued. She went on to tell him that his father's mother was dating two men at the time that his father was born. She told him that the man his grandmother claimed was his father's father was in actuality not his real father. His real father was the other man she was dating at the time. Terrence did not know what to make of this revelation and wondered why she would be giving this information to a ten-year old. Terrence's grandmother on his father's side had left for Cuba in 1912 when her son, Terrence's father, was five years old and had never returned to Santa Maria. Mrs. Jones would not have known her because she was younger than his father. She most likely heard this story through village gossip. Terrence did not know why he was being told this and simply put this information in the back of his mind. After she had shared that bit of information with Terrence, each time she saw him again, she referred to him by using one word. She always simply said, "family." Her use of this word to him made him uncomfortable and he never verbally responded, he always only nodded his head.

Terrence had heard the rumor that her deceased husband had been an obeah man and wondered if she knew that. He reasoned that if she knew so much about his father, she must have known or heard about her husband. Children in the neighborhood were taught to stay away from persons who might be involved with obeah.

There was another man in the neighborhood who made claims of being a good obeah man. His was called Dr. Dog. No one knew his real name, but he proclaimed he could work obeah and developed a clientele of persons who sought out his services. He was called Dr. Dog because all the dogs in the neighborhood barked incessantly when he walked by. He often walked with a big stick and also a large crocus bag. It was said that he would kill the dogs with his big stick and then place them in the crocus bag. After stuffing them into the crocus bag he took them to his house on lower Hawkins Street where he cooked them. It was said that he ate portions of the dogs and kept other portions in drums until they became liquefied. He used the liquefied portions in the performance of his obeah rituals.

Dr. Dog was disliked but barely tolerated by members of the Ovals community. He was stink and had sores on his legs. These sores came about because he seldom cleaned himself other than using the liquid, in which he had boiled the dogs, on his body as a method to keep away evil spirits. He was a stranger to personal hygiene.

The local boys in Ovals considered him a nuisance. Often, when they were playing cricket in the park, he would come by and ask them to spare him a minute to randomly fill out the football pools from England. Most boys would simply say no to his requests. Others would hurriedly do it so that he would not linger around the park with his foul odor. Several times it was reported that he won thousands of dollars on these pools and his name appeared in the local newspaper as a winner.

Dr. Dog was not satisfied with simply winning the football pools, he had another way of earning money. He managed to convince some people that he was a real obeah man and that he could help them to be successful in life. He claimed that he could help people to get and maintain jobs. He also claimed that he could break the negative spells that were put on persons by their enemies. He said that he had the remedy for most ailments, yet he was unable to heal the scabrous sores on his own legs.

To say that he had a clientele was not an idle boast on his part. The houses on Santa Maria were always open from daybreak. It is customary for the windows and doors of houses to be open to take in the fresh air and sunshine which were in abundance on Santa Maria. On the contrary, Dr. Dog always kept the windows and doors of his house tightly shut. You could never see inside the house from the outside. Despite the windows being tightly shut, there was always an extremely foul stench emanating from the house. His neighbors regularly complained of the foul stench to the Board of Health. Every six months, the Board of Health, would send three or four garbage trucks to his home unannounced. Invariably, when the workers from the Board of Health, accompanied by members of the police force appeared at his home to dispose of the dead dog parts and clean the house, there were always clients in his house who had come for his services. On one occasion, a lady who was a high-ranking member of her church was seen running from his house using a towel over her head to try to conceal her identity. It was reported that when the police and the sanitation workers arrived, she was in the process of getting a 'fruit bath' from Dr. Dog. The 'fruit bath' mixture consisted of boiled leaves from various plants mixed with the putrid liquid in which he had boiled the dead dogs. Invariably, when his home was being emptied of decaying dog parts, a crowd would gather to watch. Word would spread quickly around the neighborhood that his house was being cleaned and the curious would come to observe what was going on.

It took hours for them to clean his house. While his house was being cleaned, the workers were dressed in raincoats, gloves and face masks, to try as much as possible to eliminate coming in direct bodily contact with whatever he had stored in the house.

This continued until he died. At the end, he had not been seen for several weeks. Neighbors called the Board of Health because the stench emanating from his house was worse than it had ever been. It was during this raid carried out by workers from the Board of Health that his decaying body was found in his house. As they entered, they saw his body upright in a chair in state of extreme decomposition. His decaying body was ultimately placed in the garbage truck and removed. The two prominent undertakers on the island had been called to remove the body of Dr. Dog. When they were called, knowing of his reputation for filth, they refused, and he suffered the final indignity of having his body removed to the morgue in a garbage truck. The house was later condemned by the authorities and destroyed. No other house was built on the vacant land. No one claimed the land and the authorities were unable to establish if he had any relatives. He was buried in an unmarked grave in an area of the public cemetery earmarked for paupers. No one attended his burial. His body was taken to the cemetery from the public morgue, not in a motorized hearse, but in a makeshift horse and buggy. The driver delivered his body to the grave diggers who removed it from the buggy and then departed. The burial was swift.

Word spread through the neighborhood that he had died. Stories were told of the circumstances of his death. The boys in the neighborhood were now able to play cricket matches in the park without the prospect of being asked to fill out the English football pools. They no longer had to see his scabrous sores or smell the odor emanating from his body. Pedestrians were able to walk down the street past the property where he had lived without covering their noses. Residents who lived close by no longer had to call the Board of Health to carry out raids to remove the decaying body parts of dead dogs.

On Drake Street lived two brothers who excelled in sports. They inherited their sporting ability from their father who had played cricket for Santa Maria and the Leeward Islands. Their mother was a gentle woman. Her personality was directly opposite to that of her husband who was thought of as a difficult man. He was a warden at the prison on Santa Maria and he was tough. Under his tutelage, the prisoners made the cricket pitches on the island and maintained the major cricket field that was directly across the street from the prison.

Many who knew the family well said that younger son had the personality of the mother and the older son had the personality of the father. This was evident when they played cricket in Ovals. Both were very good, they were actually better than very good, they were arguably the two best players in the community. At the time, older members of the community debated who was the better player.

As a boy, Terrence had read a book, by the Trinidadian historian and intellectual, C.L.R. James. The book was entitled *Beyond a Boundary*.

The author described a young boy in his village of Tunapuna who was transformed when he picked up a cricket bat. In all circumstances he was ordinary, but except the moments that he had a cricket bat in his hands. The boy's name was Matthew Bondman, and he was a genius at batting. According to James, he wielded his cricket bat like a 'Stradivarius' violin. When he batted, adults from the community, some on foot and some in cars, stopped to watch him. When he was out, the adults left without seeing anyone else bat. Terrence realized that the same thing happened in his community in Ovals. When the two brothers batted, the adults stopped to watch. Adult neighbors around the field yelled out to other neighbors and they came out onto their galleries to watch these boys. The younger brother, the one with the personality of his mother, played the finest of delicate strokes. His off drive through the covers was delightful to see. The older brother was also delightful to watch. His batting was aggressive and he always attempted to overpower the bowlers and anyone else that he was playing against. His approach to batting was as if he was in a war and he was going to destroy his opponent. His attitude was always, 'I will be the victor and you will be the vanquished.' When he was not playing cricket, he was different, he was calm and friendly and was just one of the boys. By the time he was sixteen, he was known throughout the island as a cricket prodigy and went on to play for the island at that young age. At twenty-two he was playing for the West Indies and went on to become arguably the best batsman in world. Unlike Matthew Bondman in *Beyond a Boundary*, he developed his skill and did not fade into oblivion. The brother with the personality of his mother also played cricket for the island and also the Leeward Islands. At the same time, he played football for Santa Maria and was considered the best player on the island. Everyone expected that he would also be selected to play cricket for the West Indies thus joining his brother. No one ever doubted his skills. On the verge of being selected, he inexplicably quit playing cricket and focused solely on playing football.

The older brother became a hero to the people of the Caribbean and to the people of the countries that played this beautiful game. His prowess on the cricket field was well known, he became even more well known when he was offered over a million U.S. dollars to play cricket in South Africa and refused the offer. At the time of the offer, the system of apartheid was still the law of the land in South Africa. As a result of this practice, South Africa was isolated and not allowed to participate in international sporting events. The cricket authorities in South Africa were making attempts to once again become a part of the international cricket fraternity. Because blacks and whites were not allowed to compete against each other in sports, the conditionality of the million-dollar offer to play cricket in that country was that he would have to be designated as an 'honorary white'. The offer was offensive to him because of the conditionality attached to the offer and secondly, he would not allow himself to be used in this manner to soften the stigma of apartheid. The people of South Africa were not free, and their leader was still imprisoned because he asserted the dignity of his people.

◊◊

Chapter 6

Terrence has a sister that was fifteen months older than him. She started school before he did. When he saw that his sister was going to school on a daily basis he also wanted to go. In the afternoons, he would wait patiently under the mango tree in their front yard until she returned. The other students, who passed by after school was over for the day, would see him standing under the tree and tell each other to look at the 'shell dolly' under the tree.

Students passing by referred to Terrence as a doll. They had never interacted with persons who looked like him and it was unusual for persons who looked like him to live in this neighborhood. At four years old, he had straight hair, brown eyes and white skin. As he got older, the brown eyes and white skin remained, but his hair changed from being straight to being curly. He did not like staying at home while his sister went to school so he asked his mother if he could go to school as well. His mother said yes and so he went off to school with his sister, two weeks after she had started. The owner of the school and the headmistress, Mrs. Hughes, asked him why he was in school with his sister, and he told her that his mother had sent him to attend school with his sister. Mrs. Hughes said ok and so began Terrence's education in a school setting. The school did not have a formal name, it was simply called Mrs. Hughes School.

In school he looked different to all the other students, including his sister. He had white skin. Their partial European ancestry had caused him to have white skin. His African ancestry was barely evident if at all. Looking different would be one of the most significant aspects of his life. To live as a black person with white skin was the reality of his life. It was a role that he would navigate, sometimes graciously and sometimes not, during the course of his life. In his future, he would have to question whether or not his failures and successes were rightfully or wrongly on account of his own efforts.

None of his family members ever discussed the significance of the difficulties he might face growing up because of his appearance. He had to learn survival and coping skills on his own. He learned to stand up for himself and not back down when negative remarks were made to him about his appearance. His family members protected him from some of the negative remarks which were made by their neighbors. The local gossip which he did not know about was that he was fathered by someone other than his mother's husband who lived and worked in Curacao. The claim was that his father had to have been a white man. It was easy for him to recognize that he looked different to most of his family members and his friends. When he looked in the mirror, he saw the difference.

Once when he was thirteen, one of the boys from the community where he lived called him a 'white boy'. His response was swift and biting. He responded by saying,

'Go fuck yourself, you look like a fucking mechanic, you are so fucking dirty, you know my fucking name, call me by my name.'

He had surprised himself with his vitriolic response and the person that it was directed to was also surprised. There were countless other times where Terrence had to respond quickly and forcefully in cases where attempts were made to belittle and bully him because of his white skin. That boy that he responded to with vitriolic profanities never tried to bully him again.

In November of 1970, Terrence received a letter from St. Francis College in Brooklyn. The letter had been sent to his former address in Santa Maria. Three years before he left for New York, and before his sister had managed to negotiate their move to the United States, his sister had rented a small house for the four remaining siblings in Santa Maria. The small house was just up the street from the home of their aunt.

In January of his final year in high school, he knew that his father had filed papers for him to migrate to the United States. With this in mind, he researched colleges in the New York City and decided to apply to a small Catholic college in Brooklyn called St. Francis. After he submitted his application in March, he did not hear from the college and left for New York City in June, after he had taken his final exams with the exception of Chemistry which had been scheduled after his departure date.

Since his arrival in New York City, he was more concerned with finding a meaningful job and gave little thought to the prospect of attending college, immediately. All of that changed after he got this letter from St. Francis eight months after he had arrived.

The letter had been sent in June, but it arrived in Santa Maria, after he had left. The house was unoccupied at the time, but the postman managed to deliver it to the owners of the house who knew that Terrence had migrated to New York City, however, they did not make immediate efforts to reach him to inform him that a letter had been received for him.

It was not unusual for a person traveling to New York City to be asked by friends or family members to take articles such as letters, medicines and alcohol to other family members. This is the way that Terrence received the letter announcing his acceptance to St. Francis College for September of 1970. The letter had been delivered to the cleaners on Madison Avenue on a Saturday morning. He had first received a call from someone in the Bronx telling him that he had a letter from Santa Maria for him. Arrangements were made for the letter to be delivered that coming Saturday afternoon. He was in the cleaners when the man from Santa Maria arrived and delivered the letter. Terrence was surprised that the letter had come from St. Francis College.

He remembered that he had applied to this college. He had to remember because it was the only college he had applied to. He could not afford the U.S. $25 that each college application cost for submission, so he settled for applying to only one college.

He opened the letter and was pleased when he read the words, 'You have been accepted to attend St. Francis College.'

The letter went on to say that he would be required to register for classes and the process for registration was also delineated in the letter. The problem was that he received the letter in November, and he was supposed to begin classes in September, three months earlier.

He reasoned that he could solve this problem. He decided that he would attend St. Francis College. It was the only college that he had applied to and he was accepted. He was happy that he had been accepted because he now envisioned a brighter future for himself. He now had to solve the problem of the letter indicating his acceptance for the previous September.

He called the college and asked for the admissions office. He explained to the person who answered in the admissions office that he had received the letter late and that he wanted to start the following September. It was explained to him that they would check his application and that a call would be made back to him from their office. Two days later, he received the call from the office of the Dean of Admissions. He was given the good news that he would be granted permission to start the coming September. It was a proud moment for Terrence and his family. He would be the first member of his immediate and extended family to attend college.

He looked forward to the challenge of becoming a college student. St. Francis was a Franciscan college in downtown Brooklyn. He had attended a Catholic high school and a Catholic primary school after he had attended the pre-school run by Mrs. Hughes and he was also a Catholic. In high school, he liked his principal who had given him the impetus to believe that he was capable, but, at times, he had gotten into cross hairs with several of the religious brothers who taught at the school. He wanted simple answers to questions, but it seemed that his questions were interpreted as challenges and for anyone who has attended Catholic schools, it is known that the teachers, especially the ones who are members of a religious order, do not like to be questioned. Some viewed it as their primary responsibility to spread the Catholic faith and doctrine and being a teacher who cared about students was secondary.

In the fifteen-year history of the school, all the brothers had been white and were from North America. All the lay teachers were black and most were from Santa Maria. One of the brothers who came to the school at the start of Terrence's 10th grade year was originally from the neighboring island of Dominica. He was black. The school never had a black brother before. He had completed his college education and training in the United States like the other brothers. Upon his arrival in Santa Maria, many of the students did not know what to make of him. At first, the students took a wait and see approach to dealing with him. One thing going in his favor was that he was a very good basketball player. He was not very tall, but this was not an impediment. He was also reasonably good at soccer. Terrence saw him playing basketball before the school year started and was quite impressed with his skills at ball handling and his speed on the court.

An incident, between Terrence and this brother from Dominica, occurred during Night Study. Night Study was a period of the school day which the students attended from 7:00pm to 8:30pm. The school day was indeed long. Students attended classes from 8:00am to 1:30pm. The instructional school day ended at 1:30pm. Students who lived in the city were required to return to school for intra-mural sports from 3:00pm until 5:00pm. After sports, students went home for dinner but were required to return for Night Study at 7:00pm. Night Study was required each night with the exception of Friday. During Night Study, students were required to sit quietly while doing their homework. If they managed to complete all of their homework assignments in that time, then they were required to sit quietly and read or study in preparation for the next day.

As always, Terrence liked to sit in the front of the classroom. This was a habit that he carried from primary school through high school. It was an ordinary night where Terrence was engaged in doing his homework. This religious brother from Dominica was the class master who was assigned as the person in charge of the class. While doing his work and minding his own business, he was interrupted by the brother who offered him a piece of gum. Terrence accepted the gum and chewed it until dismissal at 8:30pm. Terrence thought nothing of it and surmised that the brother was simply being kind. Two weeks later during Night Study, Terrence was asked for his demerit card by the same brother from Dominica. A demerit was a disciplinary tool used by the school. All students were required to have a demerit card and it had to be surrendered to any school official who asked for it. If asked, you surrendered it and the teacher or school official could issue a demerit by initialing the card. Each initial was called a demerit and if a student received five demerits during the course of a week, the student was required to attend detention on the following Saturday for three hours from 9:00am until noon. For each demerit beyond five, the student received corporal punishment. Six demerits required the student to receive one stroke and seven demerits required the student to receive two strokes from the principal.

When Terrence was asked for his demerit card by the brother from Dominica, he was surprised and asked what he had done. The brother replied that he was chewing gum and that eating was not allowed in Night Study. Terrence responded and told him that yes, he was chewing gum, but he went on to ask the brother if he did not remember that he had given Terrence a piece of gum to chew in class less than two weeks before. The brother nonchalantly gave him the demerit and said,

"Well, I did not give you the piece you are chewing now."

Terrence knew that it would be futile if he argued so he handed him the demerit card. There were no other demerits on the card, so he was not worried about having to go to detention on the coming Saturday.

After the brother handed the demerit card back to Terrence, he took it and continued to do his work. After this incident, their relationship was irrevocably broken. Terrence avoided having any contact with him as much as possible. It was difficult because he was his Spanish teacher and they needed to communicate regarding the Spanish GCE exams which had to be taken before high school graduation. During the following school year, Terrence managed to keep his distance from this brother who, he believed, had issued a demerit to him unjustly and illogically. He felt that he had given him the demerit to prove a point that he had the authority do so without regard for whether or not it was just or fair. He managed to avoid another awkward circumstance with him until almost the end of the school year. One month before summer vacation, this brother told Terrence's class that he needed to speak with them about something very important to him as a brother. He began by saying,

"Students, I have been a religious brother for the past four years. I have decided that when I return to the United States this summer, I will take my final vows, which means that I will be a brother for the rest of my life. This is God's calling for me and the decision was not a difficult one."

Terrence sat in the front of the room and looked directly at him while he was speaking to the class. Terrence did not realize it, but he had developed a half smile. It was not a smile in the traditional sense indicating an exchange of pleasantries, it was really more of a smirk, indicating that he did not care or did not believe what he was hearing. The brother saw the smirk, and decided that he would confront Terrence about it,

"Why are you smiling?"

It was more than a question, it was actually a challenge and Terrence on this day, felt that he was up to the challenge. Terrence responded,

"I am smiling because I find it odd that you are merely twenty-five years old, and you are making a decision and telling us that you will be a brother for the rest of your life. It seems to me that a decision like this should not be made at twenty-five. Also, your decision has nothing to do with me, it's a private decision between you and your family and God."

The brother was not happy with the response and went on the offensive, exercising the perceived power he had as a brother. He told Terrence in no uncertain terms that he was out of line and he had no business coming to a conclusion like that about him. He went on for a few minutes, while Terrence sat quietly and took his verbal attack. He was satisfied that he had made his point clearly to this teacher who sometimes acted like a bully. He let him know that he did not care whether or not he was taking his final vows, more importantly he let him know that he was neither afraid of him nor in awe of him.

A year later, almost to the day, he told the same class which was now the senior class that he needed to speak to them about a matter that was troubling him. He began,

"As you know, last year when I returned to the United States for the summer break, I took my final vows which meant that I had committed to be a brother for the rest of my life. This year has been a difficult one for me, I have had to do a lot of soul searching. I have thought about this decision long and hard and I have spent many sleepless nights thinking about this. I have decided to leave the brothers and return to the life of being a layman. I will leave the brotherhood when I return to New York in a matter of weeks. This means that I will not return to Santa Maria for the new school term in September."

Once again, Terrence sat in the front of the room while this brother spoke. After he finished, he looked at Terrence as if expecting that Terrence would have something to say. Terrence did not say anything but his half smile, which could have been interpreted as a smirk, was evident. The brother saw the smirk but this time he did not challenge him or try to berate him as he had done before.

That September in New York, Terrence attended a party at Iona College. Iona College was a small Catholic college in New Rochelle, NY., a small city just north of the Bronx. A number of students who left his high school for college in the United States attended Iona. At the party, he saw the same brother, who the year before, had taken his final vows of chastity and who recently had left the brothers abandoning his vows of chastity, socializing and trying to pick up girls just like everyone else. The brother approached him and tried to start a conversation with him regarding whether or not he was having any success in meeting girls at the party. Terrence said hello and had a smile on his face, the smile that was really a smirk and walked away from him. He did not bother to answer his question regarding if he was having any success in meeting girls at the party.

Of the six brothers at the school, at the time, four of them were young and had not yet reached thirty. The two older brothers were in their early fifties and they served as both the Principal and Assistant Principal. All students at the school were required to attend mass at the Catholic cathedral on the first Friday of every month. On this day the students were required to wear their dress uniforms which consisted of white pants, white shirt and a dress tie which was maroon with white stripes across it. The students were not all Catholic but every student was required to attend mass on the first Friday of every month. Even though Terrence was a Catholic, he found the Catholic cathedral to be a place of contradiction and he voiced his concerns to one of the brothers during religion class.

The Catholic cathedral had names on the pews with the exception of the last four rows in the back. The names on the pews were recognizable. The names of prominent businessmen and other successful people in society were there. This included the names of several prominent Portuguese, Syrians and Lebanese. The names identified the pews that belonged to these people. This meant that when these people went to mass, they sat in the pews with their names on them. The Church gave the explanation that these people paid a fee to have their names affixed to the pews and consequently they had the right to use them. This meant that if your name was not on a pew, you had to sit in one of the last four rows in the back of the church. If by chance a person whose name was affixed to the pew and found someone else seated there, the offending person could be directed to change seats and or directed to sit in the pews which had no names.

Portuguese families had come to Santa Maria after the abolition of slavery when there was a perceived labor shortage. When slavery was abolished in 1834, most islands had a period of apprenticeship for four years. The apprenticeship period in the Caribbean was really an extension of slavery because slaves were required to work without pay for over forty hours per week for four years. This was a period where they had to be trained to be free men and women. Fortunately, Santa Maria supposedly did not have an official apprenticeship period. The slave owners envisioned that because of the small size of the island the ex-slaves would have no option but to remain working on the sugar plantations because there was no other method available to support themselves. Some of the ex-slaves did not follow the plan and left the plantations to fend for themselves and hence at times there was a shortage of workers.

Between 1847 and 1852 a total of 2500 Portuguese came from Madeira to Santa Maria as workers. They departed Madeira because of a severe famine in their homeland. After working as laborers for a short period of time many of them opened small business and quickly became a part of the merchant class.

Having the names of persons on the pews in the church did not sit well with Terrence and it seemed to be in contradiction to his faith which stipulated that all church attendees were equal in the eyes of God. The explanation given by the brothers when questioned to defend this abhorrent practice was feeble and feckless. Terrence voiced his opinion about this in religion class. Ironically, some of the boys in class with him were from families who had their names on the pews. They remained silent during the discussion and viewed Terrence as someone who wanted to take away their privilege. Others who were of the similar view to Terrence kept quiet because they did not want to be seen as troublemakers for questioning the practices of the Church. Terrence went so far as to try to organize a group of boys who would enter the church during off hours and remove all the names from the pews. Word soon got back to the brothers and the idea was scuttled because no one wanted to be expelled from school. An expulsion would have brought shame to the boys and their families. When questioned by the principal he maintained that he did not think it was fair. He was not punished perhaps because of the sincerity in his voice when he explained his position or perhaps the principal himself knew that it was an unfair practice. It was the same principal who had motivated him and encouraged him to be a better student because he had the ability to do well.

During his time at the school, he learned an important lesson about life. The lesson was that life was not fair, and you should not expect it to be.

Of all the years spent at this Catholic school, one brother in particular stood out as being significantly less than a paragon of virtue. He really had no business being a teacher and he certainly had no business being a member of a religious order. He was a brute in every sense and his behavior bordered on being hateful to the students that he taught. There are two incidents which Terrence remembered vividly. The first one was not necessarily about him and the second one was. This brother taught Physical Education to some students even though he himself was quite out of shape. On this particular day, he asked the most athletic student in class to climb up a huge tree and to tie a rope to a branch which was about fifteen feet high. Each student was then required to start from a flat-footed position on the ground and to pull himself up the rope until he reached the branch on which the rope was tied. Students were required to touch the branch and then return to the ground. The students with one exception, were all physically fit and did not display much difficulty in accomplishing the assigned task. Unfortunately, there is always an exception in every situation like this. One of the classmates was obese and it was obvious that he would have had great difficulty in climbing the rope. The teacher saw that the student could not complete the task and humiliated him by insisting that he climb the rope. The teacher himself in all likelihood could not climb the rope. This teacher continued to insist and told the student that he was a fat slob and that he made him sick.

Upon seeing this outburst from this man of the cloth, Terrence interceded and said,

"Can't you see that he is unable to do it? What is the point of forcing him when you know that he cannot do it?"

The teacher looked at Terrence and he looked back at him with anger in his eyes, his half smile which was really a smirk had been transformed into anger because he felt that it was unfair to humiliate a student this way. The irony of the situation was that Terrence and the humiliated student were not friends, it was not someone that he hung around with. He simply came to his defense because he felt that an injustice was being done to a fellow student and there was no need to humiliate the student because of his limited physical ability.

The brother did nothing to reprimand Terrence for his support of the fellow student. The same brother had verbally abused Terrence on the basketball court the previous year and accused him of making fun of someone when he did not. The incident occurred one Friday afternoon after school hours when they were playing a game of pick-up basketball. The brother came in on the tail end of a conversation and erroneously thought that Terrence was mocking one of the other brothers. Instead of enquiring, he jumped to that conclusion and started to verbally abuse Terrence. The verbal abuse was such that he yelled at him, called him names and ordered him to leave the premises of the school. This was done in front of all of his friends and others who were present. Once the order was given to leave the premises, Terrence did so without saying a word. On his way home he pondered how he could address the situation. This brother in particular often acted as if he knew everything and his mode of operating was to verbally abuse students. Terrence thought of bringing the situation to the attention of the principal with whom he had a good rapport. In the end, he decided not to address the matter, thinking that it was likely that the principal might take the side of the brother who was nothing more than a brute of a man.

A week later, the same brother called Terrence out of class and apologized to him in private about what had happened. He said that he was told by an adult who witnessed the incident that he was wrong in his assumption and he wanted to apologize. Terrence shook his hand, but he expressed no sentiments that he had either accepted or rejected the apology. He thought of this brother as a coward who had verbally abused him in public but chose to apologize in private. After that incident, Terrence found it difficult to respect him and it was obvious that he tried to avoid him during the student teacher relationship which was necessary. It was probably for this reason that he chose not to confront Terrence when he stood up to him regarding the student he was humiliating, because of his inability to climb up the rope.

The dynamics between the faculty and the students at the school were quite interesting. Students were required to take an exam to enter the school, but the school was ostensibly started as a way to educate Catholic boys, even though the school was open to and catered to boys from different religious backgrounds and also from different socio-economic circumstances. The range of students who attended the school differed in many ways. There were students who were the sons of the very rich and there were students who lived in poverty, whose parents made incredible sacrifices for them to get an education. In as much as many barriers were crossed and friends were made, it would be disingenuous to say that all the students were able to overcome the various disparities in the school setting.

There was a United States naval base located in Santa Maria and the students from the base attended this school. Most of the children of the Portuguese and Syrian families that lived in Santa Maria attended this school. The Syrian population was growing steadily since their arrival in Santa Maria. The families from the Middle East at the time were mostly from Lebanon. They started to arrive in Santa Maria in the 1920's and their population grew steadily from single digits into the hundreds. The groups from the Middle East became merchants and through sheer hard work and cunning moved into the middle and upper classes.

All the groups got along relatively well but that is not to say that there were no divisions. Problems did develop from time to time on account of race. The mid-sixties in the United States saw the advent of the civil rights movement and it affected the Caribbean islands as well. They were still dealing with the remnants of colonialism and exploitation. Televisions were new to the Caribbean. News of incidents in the United States could be heard of in the Caribbean islands daily in the news. Previously, the news could be heard on the radio, but seeing the pictures on television added a new dimension by bringing the incidents more to life. National magazines such as *Time* and *Newsweek* were also readily available. *Jet* and *Ebony* magazines which covered the black experience in the United States were also read widely by students who had an appetite for what was going on worldwide and particularly in the United States. The black power movement in the United States was followed closely in the Caribbean. One of their own, Stokely Carmichael, a Trinidadian, coined the term 'Black Power' and became a leader in the quest for human rights of blacks. Stokely Carmichael was both articulate and fearless. He came to prominence when he was still a student at Howard University in Washington D. C.

The brothers were all white with the exception of the one who had been born and raised in Dominica. He attended university in the United States and had been assigned to the school in Santa Maria. There was not an expectation in particular that he would side with black students if there was a conflict, but it appeared that he went out of his way to give the impression that there was never any racial conflict. He appeared ignorant to the fact that students were becoming aware of issues that were affecting their way of thinking. Some of the brothers also seemed to be unaware that certain things should not be said in a classroom. In 1967, the first black mayor of a major city in the United States was elected in Cleveland, Ohio and to the surprise of many, the principal, who was liked by many and liked particularly by Terrence, said that he did not know what America was coming to by electing a black mayor. In November of 1967, Carl Stokes was elected mayor of Cleveland, Ohio and the white principal of this school in Santa Maria said that to the students who were mostly black. Did he say this because he felt comfortable that he would not be challenged? Did he say this because he was a bigot? Terrence thought about what had been said and was unable to come up with a satisfactory answer. He knew that what the principal had said was not right, something was wrong with what he had said, and he was not challenged. He was not sure if the other students understood the gravity of what was being said to them. After this was said and no one challenged the remark, the principal continued with his Chemistry lesson as if it was just an ordinary day. He wondered if the principal said this because of what he had experienced in Santa Maria. Terrence reasoned that he might have said it because of his experiences in the United States. Were the victims to be blamed for their oppression or was this a way of justifying injustice? Justifying injustice was an incongruous concept and the more he thought about it the more he became confused. He had trusted this man and now he had said something publicly to his students, something that caused the trust to be in jeopardy. His consciousness had been raised as names such as Malcolm X and Martin Luther King dominated the news relative to the fight for civil rights in the United States. They were admired in Santa Maria for their bravery and the level of consciousness they brought to the table in their quest for racial and social justice.

Things were beginning to fall into place for Terrence. He completed his orientation at AT&T and was assigned to work in the Duplicating Services Department. This was totally different to the job he had in the garment district. At the job in the garment district, it was obvious that bosses did not really care about the well-being of the workers or specifically the workers who did what they considered to be menial jobs. They were content with treating the workers as less than human. In this new job, he met people who seemed to genuinely care about the persons who worked for the company. He was treated with respect even though it was obviously an entry-level position.

His first position in Duplicating Services was to deliver the completed work to all the various departments in the building. He enjoyed going from floor to floor making the deliveries and meeting new people. At lunch time, he did not have to leave the building to go to a terrible restaurant that served awful tasting food. He could eat lunch in the work-place cafeteria and additionally, he had an hour for lunch. It was a plus to be working for a company that treated him like a human being compared to the treatment he received at the previous job in the garment district.

When he was told that his salary would be one hundred dollars per week, he was happy but reflective. He remembered that when his sisters had quit going to high school in order to support themselves and their younger siblings, their salary was one hundred dollars per month in Eastern Caribbean dollars. At the time, one U.S. dollar was equivalent to two Eastern Caribbean dollars. In essence, he was flabbergasted that he would earn a salary in one week that was four times the amount that his sisters had earned in four weeks.

It all seemed like a blessing. This salary would be what he would use to pay his tuition to St. Francis College. The cost was two thousand dollars per year, and he believed that he could save enough money so that he could at least register for the first semester as a college student. More importantly, he could be a contributor to the household expenses which the family incurred. After the death of his father, the cleaners had been sold to one of the friends of their father. The money received from the sale of the cleaners was used to pay off the debt incurred from the funeral costs.

The funeral took place one week after their father had died. Because he was not a regular attendee at any church, the funeral service was held at the funeral parlor which they had hired to carry out the details of the burial. The funeral parlor was located on 125th Street and Park Avenue right next to the train station which took their passengers to Mamaroneck and Scarsdale. The same elevated train station under which the junkies and winos stood on a daily basis begging for spare change to buy lunch which was in reality to buy heroin, methadone and wine.

The funeral service for their father was held at the funeral parlor at 7:00pm on a week-day evening. A day before the funeral, he walked with his sister to Lennox Avenue and 125th Street to the male clothing shop which was located on the south side of the 125th Street. Without a fuss, Terrence tried on a black shiny double-breasted suit which the salesperson described as sharkskin. Terrence did not know what a sharkskin suit was, and he had never heard that description of a suit before. The suit fitted him reasonably well and it was purchased for him to wear to the funeral of his father that he did not really know.

On the evening of the funeral, he dressed in the newly purchased sharkskin suit and the new white shirt and black tie which had also been purchased for him. After they were all dressed, they walked down the four flights of stairs and crossed the street and proceeded to walk to the funeral parlor on 125th Street and Park Avenue. As they entered, they were greeted by the wife of the undertaker, who ushered them into the area where the funeral service would take place. Even though it was small, it was built like the inside of a church. There was an altar in the front with a podium. To the right of the podium was an organ, to the left of the podium was the coffin which bore the body of Joseph Antonio. It was remarkable that the undertaker had managed to make him look very life like and on his face were his glasses. At the time of his death, he was emaciated, and the undertaker had managed to make it appear as if he had brought him back to life. He was dressed in a suit which had been made by his own hands. The wife of the undertaker directed the children to sit in the front row directly in front of where the coffin had been positioned. When other attendees to the funeral service arrived, they came to the front by the coffin and paid their respects by standing next to the coffin for a minute or two and then expressed condolences to the children sitting in the front row.

At 7:00p.m., a man dressed as a minister, he was wearing a minister's collar, appeared and offered condolences to the children. An organist also appeared and positioned herself at the organ. The man wearing the minister's collar then began the funeral service. He preached a sermon as if he had known the family for many years. He was very complimentary to their father by saying that he had raised his children and now they were responsible adults. He went on to say that his children were a testimony to him being a good father. The minister did not know of the other six children that he had fathered and were not in attendance because they had been abandoned and mistreated like the children present. The organist added to the moment with her singing which was more like wailing. It was emotional and Terrence wondered if these people had really known his father. Later he realized that they were paid performers who did their act on a regular basis for the families of the deceased in cases where the deceased was not a practicing member of a church.

After the service, the attendees lingered for a while longer and those who were late for the start of the service offered their condolences to the children. They then walked the short distance back home to Madison Avenue and 125th Street. The next day at 10:00am, they walked back to the funeral parlor and got into a black limousine that would accompany the hearse to Linden, New Jersey where their father would be buried. It was the first time that Terrence had ridden in a limousine. He sat quietly while the driver followed the hearse, carrying the body of the father that he did not know, to its final destination.

As they crossed the George Washington Bridge to New Jersey, Terrence peered out the darkened window of the black limousine and saw the boats in the Hudson River below. He was accustomed to seeing the turquoise Caribbean Sea with its various hews of blue, now he was seeing the Hudson River and there was no comparison. The Hudson River looked dark and grey and appeared to be polluted. It was not a body of water in which he wanted to swim.

The black limousine reached the cemetery in Linden, New Jersey and pulled into the gate behind the hearse. Someone from the cemetery greeted the hearse and directed the driver to the spot where the father that he did not know would be buried. The cemetery was quite big and had thousands and thousands of head stones demarcating the graves. At the burial site, the undertaker directed the workers from the cemetery to place the coffin on the device that would automatically lower the coffin into the grave. The device was directly above the grave. This time there was no minister or person with a minister's collar. The undertaker said a few words and the children were directed back to the limousine for the journey back to Madison Avenue and 125th Street.

This was most unusual for Terrence. It was the first funeral that he attended in the United States and this was quite different to the funerals which he had attended in Santa Maria. It was unusual because they did not witness the gravediggers lower the coffin into the grave. The custom in Santa Maria was for a service to be held at the grave site and the attendees would actually be present to witness the gravediggers lower the coffin into the grave and for the gravediggers to manually refill the grave with the dirt that was dug up. It was during this time that the wailing and crying would be at its highest point. That was when the reality of the death had set in, when the coffin was lowered and covered. The finality of this action and circumstance was witnessed in Santa Maria. In Linden, New Jersey, it was different. The coffin was left on the device which would lower it into the grave after the attendees left. He wondered how it could be ascertained that the deceased was actually put in the grave if no family member was there to witness it.

As the limousine departed the cemetery, Terrence thought about whether or not he would ever visit his father's grave. After his mother's death, he visited her grave quite frequently. It had become a Sunday ritual for the children to visit her grave. While visiting her grave, he would read the headstones of the graves nearby. Sometimes they sat on the nearby graves that were sealed in concrete. He figured that the ones which were encased in concrete had no visitors and no one to bring flowers to be placed on them. At that young age, he decided that he never wanted his mother's grave to be fully encased in concrete because that would be a sure sign that no one came to visit. He told his siblings that he did not want his mother's grave to be encased in concrete and they all agreed that a section of it would be left open so that flowers could be brought and placed on it. Flowers could also be planted in this spot and thus other visitors to the cemetery would know that his mother's grave had visitors and it was not abandoned.

On the way back to Harlem he felt assured that he would choose to live a life that was different to the one his father had lived.

At his job at AT&T, Terrence met many new people who were around his age. This job was definitely not like the one he had endured in the garment district. It was comfortable for him to go to work each day. After work, he could go home and not be totally exhausted and drained from working virtually non-stop from morning until night. He could spend time with his siblings after each workday and he also had time to socialize with his new-found friends or with his old friends from Santa Maria. He found great comfort in maintaining the friendships with friends from Santa Maria, but it was also at this time that he began to realize that he would have to make choices regarding the types of activities that he wanted to be involved with. Maintaining friendships was important but staying out of circumstances, which could easily get him on the wrong side of the law, was equally important. Not only were most of his friends from Santa Maria living in the United States illegally, but many of them also chose to follow a lifestyle that could easily get them in trouble with the law. A regular past time of his friends from Santa Maria was gambling, especially on the weekends. It was not unusual for the guys to gather on a Friday night after they had all received their weekly paychecks to gamble in one of their apartments. Sometimes the gambling sessions were restricted just to persons from their community in Santa Maria and at other times, other Santa Marians who were not from their community would also be allowed into the apartments and participated in the gambling activities. Not only was it against the law to gamble, but it was also quite dangerous. On a number of occasions these gambling sessions were held up at gun point. This led to several of his friends also illegally acquiring guns. At times, they became so bold with their gambling that, they actually gambled on the stoop in front of the apartment building where they lived. One person would serve as a lookout in case the police were walking or driving down the street.

It came to a head one Friday night when his friends were gambling on the corner of Intervale and Kelly Streets in the South Bronx. A disagreement ensued and one individual jumped on the top of the car and kicked the other individual in the face. The recipient of the kick, stumbled to the ground, got up and opened the door of the car and took out a knife that was as long as a sword. Luckily, the first assailant was able to escape without being stabbed or seriously hurt by the knife even though several attempts to inflict serious bodily harm were made.

The first assailant had an older brother who lived with him. The older brother was not present at the time of the incident. Later that night when he came home, he was incensed by what he had heard and immediately went looking for the person who had chased his brother with a long knife that looked like a sword. Fortunately, he did not find the person who had chased his brother. When he went looking for this person, he was carrying a fully loaded gun which he had recently purchased from someone on the streets of the South Bronx.

Several weeks later, all the friends went to a party held on Intervale Avenue. At the party was a mix of persons from Santa Maria. Everyone was having a very good time at the party until around midnight when a fight broke out which ended the party prematurely. The fight broke out for something, which to Terrence, was trivial and inconsequential. A person who was not a member of Terrence's group was apparently ready to leave the party. The friend that he had come with most likely had too much to drink and had fallen asleep while sitting in the corner of the living room. His friend tried to awaken him so that they could leave, and he was having difficulty in doing so. Terrence's friend, the one that used the nick name Tiger, the same one who had jumped on the car and kicked the person in the face over a dispute when they were gambling, interceded and said,

"Why don't you leave him alone, he is sleeping and someone else will take him home?"

The person that this apparently innocuous statement was made to became offended and words were exchanged, and an all-out brawl ensued involving just about everyone at the party. Some were involved directly in the fight and others were trying to be peacemakers. A lady, who was trying to stop the fight, was hit by a chair. She was hit from behind. The person who hit her was the same person who used the side of the cricket bat to smash another boy in the head after he had refused to field. The assault with the cricket bat occurred in the park in Santa Maria, this new assault occurred in the South Bronx thousands of miles away in New York City. The force of the chair hitting her head, threw her into one corner of the living room and the wig that she was wearing ended up in another corner.

One of Terrence's friends pulled out a knife from his pocket and proceeded to whip open the blade which was about six inches long. Realizing that someone could be seriously hurt, Terrence grabbed the knife from the hand of his friend and in the process, he sustained a cut to his right hand. He closed the knife and tried to stop the bleeding by wrapping toilet paper around the wound. Shortly thereafter there were loud knocks on the door. The police had arrived after being called by the neighbors.

The groups that had been fighting against each other joined forces and lied to the police by saying that it was just a little misunderstanding that caused the argument and that they were all friends. They said that only two guys were fighting but the matter had been amicably resolved. The police decided not to arrest anyone but asked that the party be ended. Everyone agreed and left the party. Terrence and his friends went back to the apartment on Kelly Street where several of them lived. At the apartment, the person who had pulled out the six-inch knife was very upset and accused Terrence and others who were trying to stop the fight of doing nothing to join the fight. He did not like the fact that his knife had been grabbed from his hands and he did not get to use it. He was not appreciative of the fact that his knife, having been grabbed from his hand, saved him from doing serious bodily harm to someone. He did not seem to grasp that his knife, having been grabbed from his hand, in all probability, caused him not to suffer the serious consequences that would have ensued if he had used it to hurt someone. Terrence made it clear that he felt he had done the right thing by taking away the knife from his friend. After they had discussed the matter, Terrence left the apartment in the South Bronx and headed home to the family apartment on Madison Avenue and 125th Street in Harlem. On the train, he made the decision that he would curtail his hanging out in the South Bronx because the potential for serious trouble was becoming too evident. He wanted to maintain the friendships, but he did not want to be involved in activities that could lead to his arrest. His trips to the South Bronx became less and less frequent until he eventually just stopped going.

He did not want to be involved in any way with the police but try as he might, it seemed that the presence of the police was always a factor for young men living in Harlem. Through no fault of his own, an incident with the police could have cost the lives of Terrence and two of his friends from Santa Maria who were with him at the time the incident occurred. Two of his close friends who had moved to New York to attend college and to better their lives were with him on this Saturday morning. It was winter and they were dressed accordingly in jackets and woolen caps. Harlem on a Saturday morning was a lively place with hundreds of people on 125th Street, the most popular street in Harlem. It was Terrence's idea for them to walk to the Daitch Shopwell supermarket on 125th Street and Broadway. The supermarket was located directly under the elevated tracks for the local number one train. Terrence came up with the idea to go to this supermarket because on the previous Saturday he had gone to the Daitch Shopwell on 135th Street and 5th Avenue to see his childhood friend Tess, who worked there. When he entered, he saw a stunningly beautiful girl who was about eighteen or nineteen years old. She was working as a cashier. He asked Tess about her and was told that she was only filling in for someone who was absent and that she actually worked at the supermarket located under the subway tracks at 125th Street and Broadway. It was for this reason that he suggested to his friends that they should go there. He thought that he might see her and this time he promised himself that he would speak to her if he saw her again. The first time that he had seen her, he did not speak, even though he had planned to, when he came face to face with her at the cash register, he froze and was at a loss for words.

They were happy and full of enthusiasm as they walked along 125th Street towards Broadway. At 5th Avenue, they passed Ories Tailors that did custom tailoring. Terrence had heard his friends who had come 'through the window' and lived in the South Bronx, talk about the pants and suits which they had made there. These young men who worked in 'shipping' in the garment district often went to great lengths to impress each other and to impress other newcomers of the success they had gained in the short time that they had lived in New York City. The one way that they felt had the most immediate effect on impressing others was by wearing expensive clothes. It did not bother them that they lived from paycheck to paycheck and towards the end of each week before they were paid, they were penniless and did not have enough money for food. All was well again on Friday when they were paid. They did not even refer to it as getting paid or getting their salary. They often said, 'the eagle shits on Friday.' The first time Terrence heard that expression he did not know what it meant and looked puzzled. He was then told what it meant. It seemed incongruous at first, but he was also told that the eagle is an important symbol in American folklore. The eagle appears prominently on the American dollar bill and also appears on the U.S national emblem. The reference obviously was in connection to the eagle's prominence on the U.S. dollar bill.

They crossed Lennox Avenue and perused the books that were on display outside of the African Bookstore which was located on the northwest corner of 125th Street and Lennox Avenue. Opposite the African Book Store directly across 125th Street was the Central Ballroom, a popular dance hall frequented by many Santa Marians who had come illegally. It was here that they came on the weekends after they had received their expensive tailor-made clothes from Ories Tailors. It was this ballroom where they came to see and be seen. It was likely that they would be seen by fellow islanders who knew that they had lived in poverty in Santa Maria. Now they were able to show some trappings of success even though their tailor-made suits did not tell the story of their lives in New York City. The suits did not tell the story of them working for long hours in 'shipping' in the garment district. The suits did not tell the story of them working under less than humane conditions for companies which only considered the financial bottom line.

On the Southwest corner of 125th Street and 7th Avenue, they passed the Harlem landmark, the Hotel Theresa. It was a popular landmark in Harlem, but it became more popular and famous when Fidel Castro stayed there as guest in 1961 when he came to New York City and gave his marathon speech at the United Nations. Dressed in his military fatigues, he spoke at the United Nations and his speech lasted for four hours and sixteen minutes. Fidel Castro and his entourage had originally been booked at a mid-town hotel but when they checked in, the hotel demanded payment of cash up front, and this angered Castro and he transferred to the Hotel Theresa and said that he believed that he would get better service at this hotel in Harlem.

On their way over to 125th Street and Broadway, they passed the legendary Apollo Theatre. While growing up in Santa Maria, they had heard about this theatre as the mecca of soul music. To be successful as a soul singer you must first get the approval of the audience at the Apollo Theatre. They had seen video tapes of James Brown and Otis Redding perform here. Just weeks before Terrence had gone there to see the Queen of Soul, Aretha Franklin, and King Curtis. These were experiences that he would never forget. Harlem, at the time, was considered the center of black culture and life in the United States and he was living and experiencing it on a first-hand basis. This Saturday morning, 125th Street was alive with people going to and fro. Some were shopping for clothes and some were shopping for fruits and vegetables. There were also tourists taking in the views and sights of this city within a city.

On 8th Avenue, there were representatives of the Nation of Islam, selling their newspaper the *Final Call*. Selling was somewhat of an understatement. They were more like cajoling, convincing and demanding that you buy their newspaper. The newspaper was often thrust into your hands as if it were a gift and once you took it then the spiel to purchase it went into full effect. Sometimes it was easier to just buy the newspaper than to try to give it back to the person who had thrust it into your hands in the first place. If not, you were likely to be followed and given a lecture on the advantages of becoming a Muslim in this society and to become a practitioner of their faith whose leader was the Honorable Elijah Muhammad. They were quite convincing, not only in selling their newspaper but also in convincing you that the life and path they had chosen had brought them great fulfillment and joy. Additionally, it was difficult not to buy a newspaper from someone dressed in a suit wearing a bow tie. On this day, Terrence bought the *Final Call* and folded it and placed it in the army jacket that he was wearing.

He had bought the army jacket at an Army and Navy store on 125th Street on Lexington Avenue. These stores sold military style clothing to persons who were not necessarily in the military. Terrence had bought the jacket because he needed a jacket for the winter and these stores sold their clothing at extremely affordable prices. When he wore the jacket some people actually believed that he was in the army and that he was home after serving in Vietnam. At first, he corrected those who made comments about the jacket letting them know that he was not in the army. At the time, there were many who vehemently opposed the war and were not afraid to confront soldiers who had come back. Afterwards, he simply ignored those who made comments whether the comments were positive or negative. He had purchased the jacket and was not about to discard it because some people chose to make an issue of it. Frankly, he could not afford to buy another jacket for the winter and this one kept him quite warm.

Across the street from the Hotel Theresa, was a Florsheim shoe store. Every time Terrence passed this shoe store and other shoe stores, he would look into the window and admire the shoes that he saw. He longed to be able to go into a store like this and purchase dress shoes that he liked. He had made a promise to himself as young boy that he would buy as many dress shoes as he could afford when he was able to do so. As a schoolboy in Santa Maria, the school uniform consisted of wearing dress shoes on a daily basis. For the entire time he attended the school, he never had more than one pair of dress shoes at a time. Walking back and forth to school would cause the shoes to be worn out very quickly and sometimes his shoes would be worn out at the bottom and he had to stuff the shoes with pieces of cardboard to prevent his feet from directly touching the ground when he walked. This did not solve the problem much because the cardboard would get worn away quite quickly and the process had to be repeated. Of course, this was only a quick fix. The most difficult and embarrassing times occurred when it rained, and the rains often came unexpectedly. When it rained, both of Terrence's feet would be wet because the cardboard which protected his feet from the ground would become soaked and disintegrate. If this happened on his way to school in the morning, he would spend the remainder of the day with his feet wet in the wet shoes. At this young age, he accepted the circumstances of his poverty, but he knew that one day he would take the opportunities which might come to him and he would make the best of them. As they peered into the window of the Florsheim shoe store, he felt a sense of contentment that his shoes no longer had holes, but he knew that one day he would be able to buy as many shoes as he wanted to just to calm his mind and to soothe the hurt he felt when he wore shoes with holes in the soles and some of his classmates laughed and made fun of him.

It was difficult to endure this pain caused by him having to wear shoes with holes and caused by the insensitivity of those students who were appreciably better off than he was. Another painful memory which would be seared into his mind forever occurred on a day when he was walking home with two classmates. One of them was the son of a man who was an official in the government. This official in the government later became the Minister of Education. This man and his family, at the time that Terrence and his siblings suffered terribly from the abuse of their father, lived a few doors away from Terrence. Of course, the neighbors knew of the abuse, so it was not a secret. As Terrence and his two schoolmates were walking through Ovals, the boy, whose father would later become the Minister of Education, asked Terrence why he and siblings did not live with their father anymore. When he was asked this question, Terrence hesitated and did not answer right away. He knew that the schoolmate who asked him the question, knew the answer. Before Terrence could gather his thoughts, the questioner told the other schoolmate that their father had thrown them out of the house. Terrence did not respond but he was hurt, he felt it deeply. It was a sting that he would remember for a very long time. Afterwards he distanced himself from that schoolmate who had made him feel the pain again of his father's cruelty for no apparent reason but to be mean spirited and to humiliate him.

The three friends reached 125th Street and Broadway and looked for the Daitch Shopwell supermarket which they realized was actually on Broadway between 124th and 125th Streets. Several short blocks away on 116th Street and Broadway was the world famous, Columbia University.

As they entered the supermarket Terrence saw the beautiful girl, that he had convinced his friends to accompany him to see, at one of the cash registers checking out customers. He pointed her out to his two friends, and they agreed that she was beautiful. Now he had to figure out a way to approach her to talk to her. He figured that the easiest way to do this was to purchase three cans of Coke and to have them checked out by her. He felt that he had to at least ask for her phone so that he could chat with her away from the store. As they walked around the store, they sensed that a man was watching them intently from his perch above the cashiers. The perch was located to the right side of the cashiers so when customers were checking their items their backs were to the perch and the man observing the entire store from this elevated position.

After they were in the store for a few minutes, they heard sirens wailing outside, but they thought nothing of it. For the time that Terrence was living Harlem, he had grown accustomed to the sirens of the police cars and the sirens of the fire engines. This was a daily occurrence and nothing to be alarmed about.

They were in an aisle to the back of the store where Terrence had picked up three cans of Coke. These were the items that he would use to meet and ask for the phone number of this beautiful girl that he had convinced his friends to accompany him to see. As he was walking further to the back of the store, he heard a voice, from behind,

"Put your hands on your heads and turn around."

He looked behind and saw two policemen with their hands on their guns. There was a man next to them in the aisle and he thought that the policemen were directing their words to the man. Terrence wondered if the man had been stealing and was convinced that he was the one that the words were directed to. One of the policemen said again, this time in a sterner voice,
"I said put your hands on your heads and turn around!"

After this second order was given, still thinking that the order was not directed at them, Terrence said to the policeman,

"Who are you talking to?"

The policeman said,

"I am talking to you, all four of you."

This statement stopped them dead in their tracks because the policeman directly had said that he was talking to all of them, the three of them that were together and the man that they did not know. They put their hands on their heads as they had been directed and turned around. When they turned around, there were three more policemen with guns drawn who were facing them. There were five policemen and they looked very menacing and spoke in menacing voices. They were escorted into a back room that was refrigerated and used for packing meat. It was quite cold, appreciably colder than the temperature on the street even though it was winter.

In this refrigerated room, all four of them were searched by the policemen. The searches were quite thorough and intrusive. They were not strip searched but it was as close to that as possible without actually removing their clothes. Even their knitted caps were taken from their heads.

When the policemen carried out their intrusive search, they did not find anything in anyone's pockets other than wallets and house keys.

Surprisingly or maybe not surprisingly the policemen, New York's finest as they were called, offered no explanation regarding what had just taken place. Terrence spoke up and asked,

"What is this about, why did you do this?"

The other man that was in the aisle with them said,

"I am just here buying groceries for my family and you do this to me for no reason, these three guys know each other but I do not know them, and I am not with them. My wife is with me, she was in the other aisle with our shopping cart."

One of the policemen said to all of them,

"You can go now, the manager called 911 and said that suspicious persons were in the store and he felt strongly that you were going to rob the store."

Terrence's friends were upset, and one said,

"Let's just go, let's get out of here."

The other man said,

"This is so wrong, I could have been killed for simply shopping for my family."

Terrence went back for the three cans of coke and picked up a packet of cookies and went to the cashier, the beautiful girl that he had come to see. The cokes which he had in his hands when they were ordered to put their hands above their heads had been taken out of his hands by one of the policemen and placed on a shelf.

The manager, the man who was perched on the elevated platform, the one who had made the call to the police and said that the supermarket was about to be robbed, stood at the perch and looked on as Terrence spoke to the beautiful girl. Terrence did not have to initiate the conversation because she smiled and started the conversation with him.

"What did you guys do?" she asked.

"We did not do anything, apparently your manager thought that we were robbers, and he called the police."

She smiled and said,

"I am sorry that happened to you."

He asked her name and she smiled once again and said,

"My name is Luz Fernandez."

The opportunity was there to ask for her number and even though he had butterflies in his stomach, he summoned the courage and did it. She wrote her name and number on the receipt and he and his two friends left the supermarket.

Outside, he saw four police cars that had raced to the supermarket to apprehend the robbers or to avert the imagined robbery that was about to take place.

Neither the policemen nor the manager who had made the call offered an apology for what had happened. Four human beings had been held up at gunpoint by the policemen and this man who caused this to happen, did not feel the need to apologize. It was as if their feelings and by extension their lives, did not matter. The three friends walked back to 125th Street and Madison Avenue in less of a jovial mood than they had journeyed to Broadway to see the beautiful girl who had struck his fancy.

Terrence became friends with Luz Fernandez. When he called her the day after the incident with the policemen, she once again apologized for how he and his friends had been treated. He told her that it was not her fault and that she did not need to apologize. After he explained that they had made the journey there just because he wanted to see her again after he had seen her the previous week at the store where she was filling in for someone, she became even more apologetic. They quickly became good friends and enjoyed spending anytime they could together. When she came to meet him, she often had to have her little sister tag along. This of course was a suggestion of her mother. Her mother had brought her children from the Dominican Republic to New York City in search of a better life.

At about the time that they met, Terrence was trying to distance himself from a girl he had met shortly after he came to Harlem to live. He was in the cleaners one late afternoon when an attractive young lady came into the store with three dresses to be cleaned. The dresses were checked in and she was told that they would be ready for pick up on the next afternoon. It was almost closing time and his sister was already back from work and was in the store. She usually stayed in the store after work until closing time which was 7:00pm. After the young lady who had brought in the three dresses left the store, Terrence told his sister that she was pretty and his sister said that she behaved in an odd manner very much the way a drug addict would behave. His sister said that she fidgeted much the same way as a heroin addict would. Terrence dismissed the words of his sister because he did not notice anything to indicate that she was a drug addict. She did not have scabrous swollen arms and she did not appear to be in a daze.

The next afternoon she came back to pick up the dresses and Terrence got her dresses from the rack. She examined them and immediately pointed out that one of her dresses was missing. Her claim slip said that she had brought in three dresses and indeed there were only two in the packet. One of the dresses had not been brought back from the company which was contracted to clean the dresses. It was explained to this attractive young lady that her dress would be ready the next day. She was told that it was probably an oversight that the company had not brought it back. The next day she was back again to collect her missing dress and the dress had not yet been found. It was brought to their attention again, and they promised that it would be returned as soon as possible. They said that it was likely that the dress had been shipped to one of the several other cleaners that they had contracts with, and it would be found in a short space of time. The dress never came back, and the cleaners had to pay for the young lady's dress and then be reimbursed by the contracted dry-cleaning company.

It was a long, drawn-out process when there were lost items and the person whose item was lost only received 50% of the value of the item. This did not please customers whose items were lost, and this also did not please this young lady whose dress was lost. The only upside, if it could be called an upside, was that Terrence and the young lady became friends. He did not heed his sister's warning that she appeared to be a drug addict. Her name was Cheryl, and she was nineteen years old and had a baby that did not live with her. The baby lived at a place called the Hale House. Terrence did not know it at the time, but the Hale House was a place for babies who were born to mothers who were addicted to heroin. He simply thought that she was not capable of taking care of her child because of her young age. Cheryl lived with her aunt in a basement apartment on 129th Street and Madison Avenue while her parents and siblings lived on Remsen Avenue in Crown Heights, Brooklyn in a large luxurious house. Her father was the pastor of his own church in Brooklyn and drove a customized Cadillac Seville.

Terrence learned that Cheryl was a complicated individual with many issues that needed to be resolved but she did not know how to resolve them. As their relationship developed, she confided in him and told him things that were alien to him as a young man from the Caribbean. He first found out that she was virtually helpless when it came to doing any work in the house. She was not even able to make a cup of tea. He got first-hand knowledge of this situation when her aunt had to leave town for a few days. Cheryl was in a panic and said that she could not cook and that she had to go to a restaurant three times per day for her meals. Terrence suggested that she make her own breakfast, but she refused and said that she did not know how to cook eggs. He offered to show her how to make scrambled eggs with cheese and she rejected his offer. He then told her to boil a couple of eggs and she also said that she did not know how to do so. He gave up offering to assist in this fashion and despite the fact that she did not have much money, she went to a greasy spoon restaurant for all of her meals during the time of her aunt's absence. She could not cook, and she could not clean, but she knew about what was fashionable and what was expensive in terms of clothing and shoes. When she had to be repaid for the dress which had been lost by the cleaners, she claimed that she bought it for three hundred dollars even though she did not produce the receipt to substantiate her claim.

Terrence started off liking Cheryl, they were a cute couple, at least that is what they were told when they went out together. The liking started to turn to empathy after she had begun to tell him the stories about her family and about her son. It was obvious that she missed living with her apparent well to do family in Brooklyn. She implied that when she became pregnant, her parents were ashamed of her and suggested that she move in with her aunt in Harlem. Her father had an image to protect as the pastor of his own church. He did not want his unmarried, pregnant daughter to be seen by the members of his church.

One Sunday, Terrence accepted her invitation to attend a service at her father's church. Her father was an imposing, overweight man who preached a sermon of hell fire and damnation on that particular day. She introduced him to her mother who appeared to be a person who was quite shy and introverted. She was unlike her husband who seemed to be extroverted and not at all unwilling to show that he was in charge.

After the church service, they went to the house of her cousin who had also attended the service. Terrence was surprised that when they arrived at the cousin's house, they invited him into the basement and the two cousins immediately began to smoke marijuana. They offered him some of the marijuana, but he declined. They smoked marijuana and talked about the possibility of getting cocaine for the next time they met.

On the train ride back to Harlem on that Sunday morning, after the church service and after the visit to her cousin's house where they openly smoked marijuana and talked about acquiring cocaine for the next time they would meet, Terrence's mind was in a state of conflict. He liked her but now he felt sorry for her regarding her actions and decision making. The situation was incongruous to him considering that it was immediately after attending church that she smoked marijuana.

Two weeks later on a Saturday night, he was made aware of the full gravity of her condition. This particular Saturday evening, she called him in a panic and asked him to come to see her at the home of her aunt. He walked over to the apartment which was only a five-minute walk away. She opened the door shortly after he rang the doorbell. Her aunt was not at home when he arrived. She was sweating profusely and appeared to be in a state of desperation. She told him that her supply of methadone had run out and she was desperate for a fix. She asked him to accompany her to 125th Street and Park Avenue where the junkies congregated so that she could buy either methadone or heroin.

He felt as if he had been kicked in the stomach. He did not know that she was an addict even though his sister had suggested it when she first brought her three dresses into the cleaners. How could he say no to her now when she was in a state of desperation? He agreed to accompany her but told her that it was all he could do, he told her that he would come with her but that she would have to make the transaction to purchase either the methadone or heroin. They walked the short distance over to 125th Street and Park Avenue and lingered under the overpass for the trains which took people to Mamaroneck and Scarsdale. The same people that he had ignored on his first journey downtown to find a job, now he was among them. Luckily, she found someone who was a recovering heroin addict and received his methadone at the same clinic that she did and convinced him to allow her to buy three methadone tablets. She promised him that she would replace them when she received her own supply when the clinic reopened on Monday. Back at the apartment, he watched as she diluted one of the tablets in orange juice and drank the liquid. In about thirty minutes, she stopped sweating and her anxiety level decreased.

After she appeared calmer, Terrence left the apartment and started to walk back home. He was thinking about what he had just experienced and knew that she was making it more difficult for them to continue to be close friends. He was in deep thought and he also sensed that he was being placed in a dangerous situation. He reasoned that he would face more dangerous situations if he continued to be her friend and at the same time he felt a strong sense of empathy for her. As he crossed 128th Street, he felt uneasy and noticed that two boys were crossing the street and coming towards him from behind. One of the boys appeared to be holding a gun in his right hand. Terrence immediately began to run as quickly as he could. He did not stop running until he was safely inside the building where he lived. He had heard of others being robbed at gun point and this was a close encounter for him.

Two weeks later Cheryl called him again and asked to see him. He went to the apartment and this time she was even more distraught than the last time when she needed to buy methadone. When she opened the door, at first, she appeared calm and introspective. She said she wanted to talk. She was wearing a blue long sleeve shirt and she pulled up the sleeve on her left arm. On her arm were needle marks which formed tracks. She said that for the past week she had fallen off the wagon and she was using heroin again and if she did not get help, she feared that she would once again be a junkie. Tears came to his eyes, but he did not know what to say or do. She was asking for his help, but he did not know how to help her. It was on this night that she explained to him for the first time why her son was living at Hale House. She said that she desperately wanted to get her son back, but she knew that she would not get him back unless she was clean and totally off drugs. He nodded and realized that they were two helpless people, she, wanting help, and he not being able to give it. The only words which came to his mind to say were,

"Call your father and mother, they will help you."

This statement appeared to make her angry. She responded,

"They will not help. It is because of them that I am in this dilemma that I am facing."

Despite her statement he said,

"You should at least try."

After that, he left and went home. He did not understand how a girl like that could have become a heroin addict. She was tall and extremely attractive, she had parents who were obviously not poor and wanting for anything and here she was in a run-down basement apartment in Harlem living with an aunt and being a heroin addict. This girl who liked fine dresses and jewelry and gave the impression that she was elegant and sophisticated, was hooked on heroin, the drug that destroyed so many lives in Harlem. The evidence of the harmful nature of the drug was there for all to see but still the influence and pull of this drug could not be resisted by some.

When he arrived home, he felt sad and helpless and went to his room and fell asleep knowing that her troubles were beyond his ability to address and fix.

In the past Cheryl had spoken about her ex-boyfriend who was from Belize. She said that he was the one who had introduced her to heroin use and that they both used it together. She said that he had managed to kick his habit and he was now serving in the army in Vietnam. She said that they had broken up before he joined the army, and it was their break-up which caused him to get clean. She said that she was happy for him and wanted to use him as an example and motivation for her to kick the habit as well.

During the time of the Vietnam War, there were articles and pictures of soldiers in the New York Post newspaper, who were completing their duties and returning home.

About a month after she had revealed the needle marks on her arm indicating that she was using heroin again, Terrence was reading the New York Post. On the page, which featured returning soldiers, he saw a picture of a soldier with his helmet and M16 weapon walking through a Vietnamese village. The caption gave the name of the soldier and said that he had completed his duties and he was on his way home. Terrence recognized the name as that of Cheryl's ex-boyfriend. He read the caption again to be sure that it was the same name that he remembered. That evening, Cheryl called Terrence and asked if he had seen the New York Post that day. Terrence responded that he had read the paper. She asked if he had seen the picture of the returning soldier and he simply said yes. She went on to point out that it was a picture of her ex-boyfriend and that he was coming home.

Three weeks later while Terrence was chatting with Cheryl at her aunt's apartment, the phone rang, and she screamed when she heard the voice on the other end. Terrence sensed that it was the ex-boyfriend who had returned. She got off the phone and told him that she had to go to Brooklyn because her ex-boyfriend had returned and was now in Brooklyn. He walked her to the taxi stand on 125th Street and Park Avenue, the same place where he had accompanied her to buy methadone. She did not have sufficient money to pay for the taxi, so he opened his wallet and gave her the ten-dollar bill which he had. She said thanks and he stared at the taxi as it took off heading east on 125th Street to the East Side Highway also called the FDR drive to take her to Brooklyn. When he went to bed, he felt a sense a relief, he felt that a heavy weight had been lifted from his shoulders.

The next time he saw her it was a month later walking on 125th Street and 7th Avenue with her ex-boyfriend who seemed to be her boyfriend again or at least her partner in heroin use. Both were heavily under the influence of drugs. Each had a dazed look and he was scratching himself when they walked by. Two weeks later Cheryl called Terrence and asked to see him. He told her that he was busy and that he would call her back when he was free. He never called her back as he had promised. Surprisingly, after he did not return her call, she showed up unannounced at the apartment he shared with his siblings. He was sitting with his friend Luz Fernandez in the living room and did not hear the doorbell. His sister came and told him that the doorbell had rung, and she had looked through the peephole and saw that it was Cheryl. He told his sister to tell her that he was not at home. When told he was not at home, she left. He never saw her again.

His friendship developed with Luz and he was happy to learn that her physical beauty did not surpass her beauty on the inside. She was from the Dominican Republic and had moved to New York City with her family before she was a teenager. She lived with her mother and sisters in the Dominican community on the upper west side of Manhattan.

◊◊

Chapter 7

Terrence worked at AT&T until August of 1971 and started attending college in September of that year. His employment at AT&T was rewarding. In the short time that he worked there he had been promoted and given a substantial raise. In his first two months of employment, he had been given a raise and new responsibilities. He no longer had to deliver the finished work to the various departments in the building. He was trained to work on one of the new duplicating machines and at the end of his training, even though he was still relatively new and there were other employees with seniority, he was given the assignment to work on this machine. This new assignment came with a raise and he was now earning $125.00 per week.

When the time came for him to resign, he contemplated keeping the job and going to college on a part-time basis. This would have taken him a much longer time to get his degree. He reasoned that he wanted to be a regular full-time college student and that he needed to make the sacrifice to pursue his dream of getting a college degree. The problem was that he was making a substantial amount of money and he was not sure that he would make that much even when he graduated from college.

He had not made a decision on the course of study that he would pursue. He had no real guidance of what was available to him. In Santa Maria, the students were taught to prepare for the annual Cambridge O Level Examinations and not much after that. College was not affordable for 95% of the students and it was not a consideration.

He made the decision that he would resign and attend college on a full-time basis. On the day that he went to register, he was given a list of suggested classes for freshmen and used that as a guide. He registered for five classes for the fall semester of 1971. He would be taking five classes that amounted to fifteen credits. He brought home the registration package for the classes and showed it to his siblings. He was excited about this new journey of his life, but he also knew that he would have to now go out to find a part-time job because he still had to support himself. He decided that he would wait until after his classes had started before applying for a part time job. This was to make sure that he could handle the workload of his classes and hold a job at the same time.

One of the required classes that he took during his first semester was U.S. History of the 20th century. This was the only one of his five classes that he found to be difficult. Having not taken any classes in U.S. History before, he found that he had to spend more time to familiarize himself with the concepts of how the American political system worked. In Santa Maria there were no classes in U.S. History or World History. They were taught a version of Caribbean History which was not really Caribbean History at all. They were taught all about jolly ole England and their marauders who were pirates, slave traders and slave smugglers in the Caribbean. They were taught about Sir Francis Drake, Admiral Lord Nelson, Sir John Hawkins and others. In addition to not being taught the real history of the Caribbean, they were taught Caribbean History by one of the newly arrived brothers from New York who did not know anything at all about the Caribbean much less its history. His knowledge of the subject was limited and was acquired when he picked up a Caribbean History book for the first time after he received the schedule of the classes, he would be teaching several days after he arrived in Santa Maria. His teaching of the subject centered around him reading the chapter before it was assigned to the students. In class, the students were required to read the chapters and to answer the questions posed at the end of each chapter.

Terrence's only consolation in this U. S. History class was that the other students from the Caribbean appeared to be having difficulty as well. He dutifully read all the assigned readings but during class discussions, he found that he still had not grasped all the concepts that were being discussed. During a classroom discussion of the second World War, he did not know of the circumstances of the Japanese bombing of Pearl Harbor. During his high school years, one of the brothers carried out what he called Japanese inspections of their uniforms. This meant that their teachers carried out unannounced inspections of their uniforms and if they were not wearing their uniforms in the proper way, they would receive demerits for the infractions. A particular area of concern for the teacher was that their shoes had to be shine. Terrence found it difficult to keep his shoes shine because they were already in a state of disrepair, but he tried as best as he could so that he could avoid getting demerits. He had to keep them up to the standard required by this teacher who seemed to take joy in issuing demerits to students after carrying out a Japanese inspection. In his freshman U.S. History class, he learned that the Japanese attacked the U.S. ships in Pearl Harbor during a surprise attack which resulted in an escalation of the war and the ultimate dropping of the atomic bomb on two Japanese cities, Hiroshima and Nagasaki.

At the Catholic elementary school that he attended in Santa Maria, the students were shown the movie, *Heaven Knows Mr. Allison*. This movie was about a soldier and a nun who were stranded on an island in the Pacific. Ostensibly, they were hiding from Japanese soldiers who had taken over the island. This film might have been about religion and the war, but the students who saw it at the age of eight or nine had absolutely no idea what it was about and ironically it was shown every year around Christmas time. Subliminally, it showed one American soldier and an American nun, single handedly outsmarting a troop of Japanese soldiers and in the end being heroically saved by a troop of American soldiers, who had returned to the island on which they were previously stranded.

In this U.S. History class, he learned about the history of segregation and how it came about. He already knew about the civil rights movement of the sixties, but he did not know about the foundational circumstances that had been fought in the courts. He learned of the terms, 'separate but equal', 'all deliberate speed' and 'all men are created equal'. These phrases were confusing to him in their interpretation. The term 'all men are created equal' seemed to be very straight forward in the literal sense. If the people of the United States believed that statement to be true, then there would not have been a need for the Civil Rights movement or the 14th Amendment to the U.S. Constitution in 1868 which stated that 'no state shall…deny to any person within its jurisdiction the equal protection of the laws'. Terrence asked his professor about this,

"If the American people truly believe in the words of the 14th Amendment, then how could the Supreme Court uphold the concept of 'separate but equal' in 1896, twenty-eight years after the 14th amendment came into effect. Furthermore, I don't understand if we agree that 'all men are created equal' as is stated in the 'Declaration of Independence' in 1776 why was there a need for Plessy v. Ferguson in 1896, one hundred and twenty years later. And why was there a need for Brown v. Board of Education in 1954? Weren't the protections guaranteed by the Constitution in place and implemented?

The professor answered by saying,

"There are different interpretations to each statement, and it is up to courts to decide. And even when the courts decide there are often variations how the rulings are implemented."

The answer left Terrence more confused than before. Why does a court have to decide if 'all men are created equal?' The answer appears to be self-evident and does not seem to require any interpretation. He wondered if the explanation was a deliberate effort to confuse the students. Terrence also asked his professor,

"Can you also please explain what it means by 'all deliberate speed' as ruled by the court in 1955 regarding Brown v. Board of Education. I looked up the words deliberate and speed in the dictionary and they seem to have different meanings. Deliberate means with care and speed means the opposite. So how could they integrate the schools with deliberate speed?"

The professor said,

"I think they meant to do it carefully."

Once again, his answer did not clarify or explain the dilemma that Terrence was having with trying to wrap his mind about the concepts of these terms.

Terrence wondered if the Supreme Court deliberately tried to give the school districts that were practicing segregation, a way to ignore their ruling. What would have been their purpose in doing that when they could simply have ruled in favor of the defendant school board in this case? Did they make the ruling with the full understanding that it was only a matter of time that 'separate but equal' would not find a comfortable place in American society and were giving the school districts time to fix it? Did they not recognize that giving them time to fix it, could have been interpreted by the defendants that they did not have to do it all?

He managed to get a C in the class, and he was happy. He was happy for the C, but he was not happy that he left the class with more questions than answers regarding how the courts worked and whether or not there was an overall belief in the simple term 'all men are created equal'.

He had made a few new friends in the first weeks that he attended St. Francis. He met a fellow student named Ira from the neighboring island of St. Kitts. St. Kitts and Santa Maria were rivals in just about everything. Their rivalries in sports, particularly, football and cricket were legendary. It was not unusual for a team from Santa Maria, playing a sporting event in St. Kitts to be assaulted after the game. The same thing would happen when a team from St. Kitts played in Santa Maria.

St. Kitts had monkeys and the people from this island were derogatively called 'monkey chasers'. Santa Marians were derogatively called 'garats'. Despite all of this, Terrence and Ira met, and they immediately became friends. Both of them had much in common and both discussed the possibility of becoming teachers.

They were both pleased that there were quite a number of students from the Caribbean attending this college. Some of the students were new to the United States and some actually had migrated sometime before with their families and had completed high school in the U.S. Additionally, there were several students who were from Africa, particularly Nigeria. They would tell stories that they were princes and royalty back in Nigeria. Not many people believed them, but their stories were interesting. The remainder of the school population, which was 2500, were white students from various parts of New York City, the majority from an area in Brooklyn called Bay Ridge and some from the Boroughs of Queens and Staten Island.

During their first semester, they were invited to become members of the Afro-Caribbean Student Association of St. Francis College and they did.

At the time, this organization had as its president a student from Trinidad. He wore a large Afro haircut that made him appear taller than he was. He went by the name Moringa, even though everyone knew that it was not his real name. Terrence wondered why he gave himself the name of a plant that grew in Santa Maria and most of the other Caribbean islands. He wondered if he knew that the moringa plant was also called the Tree of Life and it was said to have tremendous healing and medicinal properties. In Santa Maria, it was often used to make tea.

Terrence was not sure of the purpose of the association, but he viewed it as a way in which the Caribbean students could gather and meet to discuss matters that were of concern to all of them. Terrence thought that Moringa, as he insisted on being called, was quite forceful in some discussions. There was a time when a Puerto Rican tried to join the association and Moringa was opposed to allowing him membership. He gave a long speech questioning why the Puerto Rican student wanted to join. He was adamantly opposed to it and suggested that the student could not be trusted. He went so far as to suggest that the student could have been an informer. Terrence wondered what the student could inform about and to whom. He did not detect that they would be talking about anything of consequence which someone might want to inform others about. He viewed Moringa as a bully who wanted to get his way and he was outspoken in expressing his views as bullies usually do.

Terrence had a Spanish class with Moringa and became less impressed with him when he realized that he did just only enough to get by. This Spanish class was taught by Professor Alegre. Dr. Alegre was odd in many ways. One day when he felt that the students were not putting forth their best efforts, he proceeded to berate them and said,

"Why are you motherfuckers here wasting my time? You are just here spending your parents' money. You should be in Vietnam getting your asses shot at. Stop being pussies, do your work or go join the fucking army."

Terrence was shocked that a college professor would speak this way to his students. After class that day some students spoke about what the teacher had said but Terrence said nothing. At the beginning of the next class someone from the administrative offices came to class and asked the students to write a statement regarding what had happened. Apparently, some students had complained to the Dean about the outburst of Dr. Alegre. At the end of the semester, no one saw him at school again. It was assumed that his outburst got him fired. Some students opined that maybe he had just quit. Terrence wondered if he was one of the students who caused the professor to have this profanity laced outburst. He had taken Spanish in high school and was at the time getting a very good grade in the class, so he was not sure. He thought for sure that Moringa was one of them who provoked Dr. Alegre's ire.

St. Francis was a commuter college meaning that all the students lived away from the campus. There were no dormitories. Most of the students lived at home with their parents and families and commuted to campus on a daily basis.

Two months after starting classes in the fall, Terrence found a part time job with a bank located on 145th Street and St. Nicholas Avenue in upper Manhattan. This job was very helpful in allowing him to do his schoolwork without much stress on his time. His job required him to be at work at 4:30pm each weekday. Once he arrived, he then walked with another employee to deliver paperwork to another bank three blocks away. Upon returning, he was required to deliver additional paperwork to the main office located at Lexington Avenue and 42nd Street. After this, he was free to return home. He spent many hours per day on the subway.

Each day he left his home in Harlem at about 8:00am to arrive in Borough Hall, Brooklyn, the location of his college before his first class started at 9:00am. He remained at school until 3:30pm and then took the subway to 145th Street and St. Nicolas Avenue. Then it was back to Grand Central Station before heading back to Harlem by around 7:00pm each weekday.

One evening, as Terrence was heading home on a crowded subway train, he saw a man that he recognized. Their eyes met and the man looked away, obviously, not wanting to be acknowledged. The man had reasons why he did not wish to be acknowledged. He had been a prominent figure in not only Terrence's community but throughout the entire island of Santa Maria. This man was head of the choir at the Catholic church that they both attended. During mass on Holy Thursdays, his feet were washed by the priest as an example of how Jesus washed the feet of his disciples in the town square. The prominent positions he held in the church and in the community were well known. He was the president of the local chapter of the Jaycees and also one of the vice presidents of Jaycees International. He was a scout master and an instructor of ballroom dancing.

The year after Terrence graduated from high school the man left Santa Maria abruptly. It was learned that he was about to be arrested by the police for theft. He had been working for a company owned by one of the Lebanese families. He was trusted by them and held a position in their accounting department. During an audit, it was discovered that hundreds of thousands of dollars had been stolen and the evidence of the theft lead to this prominent man. Instead of facing the music regarding what he was accused of doing, he fled the island in disgrace.

Terrence thought nothing of seeing this man on the subway. What he had done was not the most unusual thing. Others, that he was aware of, had done similar things and had also fled the island in disgrace before the police arrested them. One such person worked at a bank in Santa Maria and had a high-ranking position. He was also the person who could be counted on to wear the very best suits and to have the most fashionable American car. The year before he fled the island to the United States, he was driving a new Thunderbird which had been imported to the island. It was the only car of its kind on the entire island. After he fled, the car sat in front of the home of his parents for a long time before it was seized by the police. It was placed in the police compound where it stayed and rotted for several years.

There was another young man that was called Shugs who also found himself in similar difficulty while working at a bank. He had started off as teller and worked his way through the ranks and then held a supervisory position in the loans department. It was found out that many of the persons for whom he had approved loans were defaulting on their loans. A further check revealed that he had fabricated the names of many individuals and received loans in the fabricated names and pocketed the money. Before he could flee, he was arrested and served two years in prison for fraud. The day after he was released from prison, Shugs took a British Overseas Air Corporation (BOAC) flight to London and never returned to Santa Maria.

When Terrence began his second year at St. Francis, to his surprise, he had as a classmate, the man who had his feet washed by the priest during mass on Holy Thursdays. The same man who, it was alleged, had stolen a large quantity of money from the company owned by the Lebanese family for which he worked. The same man who fled Santa Maria in disgrace, one step ahead of the police who were about to arrest him. The man he had seen on the subway who did not wish to be acknowledged. They were now classmates in speech.

This man seemed decidedly out of place on this college campus in the fall of 1972. In the first instance, he was about 15 years older than most of the other students. Secondly, he wore a collared shirt with a tie and a jacket to class each day. He looked more like one of the professors, he actually looked more like a professor than the professors themselves.

After he had given a speech in class one day, the professor whose surname was Monaghan told him that he made him uncomfortable. The entire class was taken aback by what Professor Monaghan had said, but he went to explain by saying,

"You are too rigid in the delivery of your speech. You are dressed in a shirt and tie with a jacket, this is very unlike college students today. You do not smile and you do not appear to be happy or sad. You do not seem to have any joy in what you are doing. Show some emotion when you give a speech, show some emotion when you are involved in discussions in class."

Of course, Professor Monaghan knew nothing about this man's past in Santa Maria, but the man knew that Terrence knew. He knew that Terrence knew because Santa Maria is a small place and when things like this happened, especially to a prominent person, the news spreads very quickly and it also spreads to other Santa Marians living in other parts of the world. He also knew that Terrence knew because of an incident that occurred a few days after he showed up at St. Francis as a student.

After Terrence saw him in class for the first time at the start of the semester, Terrence had told his friend, Ira, from St. Kitts about him. Terrence told his friend about the nefarious deeds he had done and about him fleeing from the consequences of his actions just one step ahead of the police.

The students from the Caribbean utilized an area designated as a study hall on the first floor. During times when they did not have classes, the students from the Caribbean could be found in this area or in the cafeteria. This man who had fled from Santa Maria did not hang out in the cafeteria, but he did utilize the study hall. It so happened that another student from Santa Maria attended St. Francis. One day, Terrence was in class but his friend from St. Kitts, the other Santa Marian and the man who had fled were sitting at the same table in the study hall. The man was sitting at the end of the table and was not speaking to the two others. Terrence's friend from St. Kitts was chatting with the other Santa Marian and said,

"Hey man, Terrence told me that there is a big shot man attending St. Francis now who stole a lot of money in Santa Maria and had to run away to New York."

Before he could properly finish his sentence, the friend from St. Kitts received a swift kick under the table and a nod of the head, indicating that the person sitting at the end of the table was indeed the man that he was talking about. The man continued to read his book but got up soon afterwards and left. He was never seen in the study hall again. After he left, the two had a laugh about the incident and Terrence's friend from St. Kitts offered an apology for putting him in an awkward circumstance. Later when Terrence arrived, he was told what had happened. The next time Terrence saw the man in his speech class, this man was decidedly stiffer than usual.

It was odd to pretend that they did not know each other. In addition to being a prominent member of the church they both attended, he was the one who had his feet washed by the priest during mass on Holy Thursdays and he was the head of the choir, he had also been Terrence's scout master and he was the one who taught Terrence's high school graduating class the fundamentals of ballroom dancing in preparation for their graduation ball. He was also the reason that Terrence left the boy scouts. He was an unreasonable disciplinarian who was cruel at times. One hot Saturday morning, this man led his boy scout troop on a four-mile hike to the beach. All the scouts were happy when they arrived at the beach and thought that they could immediately cool themselves by going for a swim. Instead of allowing the scouts to swim, he required them to pitch the tent while he sat under a coconut tree, refreshing himself by drinking a coke. One of the boys protested having to pitch the tent while he sat under a tree and he immediately sent the boy home by himself. This boy who was twelve years old at the time, had to make the four-mile trek back to his home because he had dared protest the orders of this man. After this incident, Terrence no longer wanted to be a boy scout and he quit. The boy who was sent home also quit.

This man taught ballroom dancing and through the church, volunteered to teach the graduates the fundamentals of ballroom dancing in preparation for the graduation ball. Once again, this man was as rigid as could be. Terrence knew that he was leaving for New York City several days before the graduation ball was being held. Because of this, he was not as serious as he should have been. He went to the practices mostly to be with his friends and to socialize with the girls from their sister school with which they had teamed up to have the ball. This man, seeing that Terrence was socializing more than he was practicing, proceeded to yell at him and told him to leave the practice and not come back. Five years earlier he had sent home one of the scouts from the beach and now he was dismissing Terrence from the practice for the ball. Even though Terrence was a bit embarrassed by being dismissed, he viewed it as no big deal because he could not have attended the ball anyway. Terrence's flight to New York was scheduled for Thursday, June 18th, 1970 and the graduation ball was scheduled for Saturday June 20th, 1970.

After all of his prominence and pompousness in Santa Maria, they were now equals in college. Well maybe they were not equals because not many other students liked this man on account of his stuffy behavior and it appeared that his humiliation, having stolen a large sum of money and having to flee the island, was not sufficient for him to demonstrate humility in his interactions with persons he came in contact with in college. He acted as if he was not aware that people knew what he did. He might have been in denial.

He abandoned his wife and two young children in Santa Maria. He had caused them an enormous amount of embarrassment because of what he had done. And now, here he was in New York City pretending as if nothing had happened.

Terrence had finished his first year and started his second year. During his first year, he worked at the bank on 145th Street and St. Nicholas Avenue. Now during his second year, he recognized that he had to find a new job because he was not making enough to support himself and to save money for the remaining years. He found it necessary to resign.

He took another job at a bank on Wall Street working from 5:00pm to 10:00pm each weekday. This job also was not sufficient so he decided that he would drive a cab on the weekends. He applied for and obtained his hack license. A license to drive a yellow cab in New York City was called a hack license. To get this license he had to get an examination by a doctor to certify that he was in good physical shape. The process of getting the physical was somewhat amusing. The doctor who carried out the physical examination was not in the best of health himself. He looked rather ill and behaved in a manner which illustrated his old age. It appeared that he could barely see and hear. The extent of the examination was simply asking Terrence to cough. He then wrote that Terrence was in good health when in fact he did not really examine him at all. The doctor sat behind a desk and told Terrence to cough and that was it. The examination was over. Terrence had been deemed as physically fit to drive a yellow cab in New York City. An assistant was in the office with the doctor, and it was the assistant who filled out the necessary paperwork and the assistant directed the doctor to sign it.

With obtaining his hack license he got a job, a position with a cab company on 6th Street and 4th Avenue in Brooklyn. Terrence was now attending classes full time, working twenty-five hours per week at a bank and driving a taxi for eight or nine hours per day on the weekends. Here he was, working over forty hours per week and attending college on a full-time basis. He had no time for socializing or spending any quality time with friends or family members. He kept doing this knowing that it would not last forever. It was a sacrifice that he was willing to make believing that he would reap the benefits in the future.

During this time of driving a New York City yellow cab, he met many other drivers who were never reluctant to offer unsolicited advice. One man in particular who worked for the same cab company would always say to Terrence,

"Look at my hands, these hands have sent my sons to university, I have three sons, one is a doctor and two are lawyers."

He would continue,

"Terrence, don't do this forever, get your education and make something of yourself. I did not get an education, but I was able to make sure that my sons did."

His hands were callused from holding the steering wheel of a cab for eight hours per day, five days per week, for fifty weeks of the year. He would lament that he did not know when he would retire. He had been driving a cab around NYC for almost forty years. He said that he knew every corner in the five boroughs of NYC.

The cab drivers that Terrence would meet at Kennedy and La Guardia Airports were the most entertaining. The time between fares waiting at these airports on certain days could be thirty minutes to forty minutes long. Terrence always had his school books with him and tried to use this time to sit in his cab and study but oftentimes he would be interrupted by other cabbies who wanted to talk and regale each other with grandiose and embellished stories of their interactions with passengers.

Some of the passengers that Terrence picked up were quite odd and others were kind and normal as expected. One passenger travelling downtown, pointed out other cars and demanded that Terrence speed up and pass them. The passenger just randomly selected cars traveling in front of them and demanded to pass them. Terrence refused and indicated that it was not safe to drive recklessly in mid-town Manhattan on a workday. The passenger became more irrational and flustered. At his destination, he refused to give a tip because his directions were not followed. Terrence was not concerned about the tip; he was just happy that the passenger was leaving his cab.

Another irrational passenger caused Terrence to be involved in an accident. The passenger was picked up on 57th Street and Lexington Avenue and wanted to go to the New York Athletic Club located on 59th Street and Columbus Circle. This passenger claimed to be in a hurry and demanded that Terrence take him there as fast as possible. During the trip, he repeatedly told Terrence that he was driving too slowly and demanded that he drive faster. When they arrived at the destination, the passenger threw the money into the fare box and opened the door without looking. As he was exiting, another cab struck the door, almost hitting him in the process. He was startled and sat in the back of the cab in a panic until the cops arrived. When they did, he claimed that Terrence did not pull over to the curb far enough to avoid the accident. Fortunately, the police told him that it was his responsibility to look before opening a door on the street side with oncoming traffic. He was also told that he should have exited the cab on the other side. He was told that he was the cause of the accident. Neither Terrence nor the other cab driver was found to be at fault and no tickets were issued. The door of the cab was bent from the accident and Terrence had to return the cab to the company and consequently lost a day of work with no pay because the accident occurred shortly after he had started his shift for the day.

Driving a cab was no easy task. Terrence learned to maximize his time to his benefit. He learned that the cab company for which he worked encouraged the drivers to work longer hours which made more money for the company and the cab drivers. After Terrence finished working at 10:00pm at the bank on Friday nights, he would pick up the cab. This was ideal time to get fares wanting to go to parties and social functions on a Friday night. He would drive the cab until 3:00am the next morning, which was the time that persons were finished partying for the night. He would go home with the cab and then sleep until 7:30am and then begin driving again. On Saturday mornings, he had a few regular customers who wanted to be taken to the supermarket or the vegetable stands to do their shopping. The cab would be returned by 4:00pm on the Saturday afternoon. He would then return home to sleep until around 9:00pm and collect the cab again by 10:00pm. He would work again until 3:00am and go home to sleep and would be up early the next morning to take his regular customers to church. He did not maintain that heavy schedule each weekend, but he did it at least once or twice per month.

Terrence worked as a New York City taxi driver for two years during his second and third years of college but stopped at the start of his senior year. He was working too much, and it began to take its toll on him. At one point he noticed that he was becoming sick quite often and when he went to the doctor, he was told that he was suffering from exhaustion that caused a weakened immune system. With a weakened immune system, he was getting colds frequently. He resigned as a cab driver because he wanted to do well during his senior year and felt that not working so much gave him a better chance of excelling academically. He had been on the Dean's List for academic excellence during his junior year and wanted to receive the same honor during his final year.

Terrence's years at college were rewarding. He learned a lot in his classes. He was particularly impressed with a book he read by Henry David Thoreau, entitled, *Walden.* In that book, was also an essay entitled, *The Duty of Civil Disobedience.* He read and reread that essay at least ten times. Thoreau's position on slavery was particularly interesting to Terrence. Thoreau felt no allegiance to a country or government where the institution of slavery was legal. It was said that when he was imprisoned for refusing to pay his taxes, when asked why he was in prison, he asked in return,

"The question is not why I am imprisoned, the question for you is why aren't you here."

He was released after a friend paid the taxes which he owed. Thoreau's basic premise was that citizens had an obligation not only to oppose injustices carried out by the government but to refuse to participate in activities such as paying taxes which allowed the government to carry on its unjust practices. He lived frugally and intentionally did not have many possessions. Accordingly, the government would not have much to take away from him in the form of punishment for refusing to pay taxes.

He built his cabin at Walden Pond where he lived for two years for the sum of $28.50. He gave the reason why he went to live at Walden Pond,

"I went to the woods because I wished to live deliberately, to front only the essential facts of life, and see if I could learn what it had to teach, and not, when I came to die, discover that I had not lived."

Terrence repeated the last line in his head over and over, 'when I came to die, discover that I had not lived.' He examined the meaning of those words. He imagined that the words meant different things to different people, but to him it meant that one should live life to the fullest. But what did living life to the fullest mean? Did it mean obtaining riches and becoming wealthy? It did not mean that to him. Did it mean living a life of purpose? What was a life of purpose? Terrence realized that he could not answer the question directly, it was something that he had to study and think deeply about.

Another of Thoreau's quotes for which Terrence sought meaning and clarification relative to his own life was,

"Most men lead lives of quiet desperation and go to the grave with the song still in them."

This, he thought, meant that most men live unfilled lives and die without having taken that major step for them to accomplish their goals because they could not visualize their own success, or they were afraid to do what was necessary to accomplish their goals. Terrence decided then that he did not want to lead a life of quiet desperation. He decided that it was within him to make goals and to do all in his power to accomplish them. Not only would he write his own song, but he would also sing it before he died. He would sing it for others to hear, not literally, of course, because he knew that he had a terrible voice for singing and could not hold a note if his life depended on it.

"Why should we be in such a desperate haste to succeed and in such desperate enterprises? If a man does not keep pace with his companions, perhaps it is because he hears a different drummer. Let him step to the music he hears, however measured or far away."

It was this quote by Thoreau that convinced Terrence to major in English Literature and Teacher Training. Despite many of his friends majoring in business and accounting with plans to work on Wall Street, where they would make substantial sums of money, he decided that Wall Street was not for him. His thinking was more in line with Thoreau's thinking. His goal was to be successful but at the same time he did not see success as simply being financially successful. He felt that he could also be successful by helping others or by service. He had heard the saying and believed that service to others was the rent that we pay for our time on earth.

Martin Luther King's role in the Civil Rights Movement was well known and he had become a martyr who gave his life for the cause. His tried to accomplish this through the use of civil disobedience. The civil disobedience espoused by Henry David Thoreau over one hundred years earlier.

Terrence learned that Mahatma Gandhi of India also was a disciple of Thoreau and used Thoreau's concept of civil disobedience in his quest to successfully gain India's independence from Britain in 1947. Prior to moving back to India after sojourns to England where he studied law and moving to South Africa to work, he utilized the concept of civil disobedience in South Africa which had a sizeable Indian population. He advocated for the rights of his fellow Indians. Indians arrived in South Africa in the 1860's and settled in Natal. Gandhi arrived in Natal in 1893 and subsequently took up the cause for Indians to be treated fairly in a non-discriminatory manner. He used civil disobedience as a tool to fight the system in South Africa which did not offer rights to Indians.

At the time, black South Africans did not receive any benefits that were given to whites. It could be argued that black South Africans were treated in a more discriminatory manner than the relatively newly arrived Indians who had come to Natal as indentured servants. Terrence viewed it as ironic that Gandhi fought for the rights of his fellow Indians who were being discriminated against, but he did not fight for the rights of black South Africans. In his writings and appeals to the authorities, he made it clear that he did not support rights for blacks. It is recorded in his writings that he referred to black South Africans as 'kaffirs', a derogatory, racially insensitive term. After finding this out about the man credited with standing up to the British and gaining independence for India, Terrence was less impressed with him. He wanted rights for his own people but not for all the oppressed. It was hard for him to imagine how someone like Gandhi could compartmentalize his feelings about different human beings in this manner.

It was at about the same time that he discovered the writings of Thoreau that he also discovered that there was a connection between the venerable Harvard Law School and his island of Santa Maria. The irony of this connection is startling because Thoreau gave lectures at Harvard in opposition to slavery which he viewed as an unjust system upheld in the Constitution of the United States of America. Harvard Law School's seed money was donated by Isaac Royall Jr., a slave plantation owner in Santa Maria. He sold a portion of his slave plantation called Royalls Estate located in the north of island and donated the proceeds to Harvard University to fund Harvard Law School.

In 1736, Isaac Royall Jr. ordered the murder of his slaves who were involved in the planning of a revolution in Santa Maria. He ordered the seventy-seven slaves involved to be burned to death. The planned slave revolution was led by King Court.

Had this revolution been successful, Santa Maria would have become the first nation with black leaders in the western hemisphere. This would have happened before black Haitians, led by Toussaint L'Overture, had their revolution and kicked out the French in 1791.

Haiti has suffered and still suffers for their success of ridding themselves of the French that occupied them. Because of their success, France was able to convince other major countries to join forces with them to bring the revolutionary Haitians to their knees economically. They were forced to pay exorbitant sums of money to the French government for their property lost or face being attacked by allied forces. Their property lost was mainly slaves who freed themselves. This economic sabotage of Haiti lasted for over one hundred years.

The irony of African slavery in the Caribbean was that it was first suggested to use African people as slaves for the cultivation of the land in Hispaniola, the landmass that makes up Haiti and the Dominican Republic, by Bartholomew de las Casas a Catholic priest from Spain. A man of the cloth made the recommendation to enslave other human beings. He was an owner of slaves who were the indigenous people of the Caribbean, he empathized with the indigenous people after having slaves of his own and made the recommendation to the Spanish Court to introduce Africans as slaves.

When Terrence became aware of this, he questioned his faith in the Catholic Church. He was a Catholic who had gone to Catholic schools for most of his life and it appeared to him that the Catholic Church had condoned and promoted slavery in the Caribbean.

Shortly after King Court and his rebels were murdered, Isaac Royall Jr. moved his family to Massachusetts, the state from which his father originated even though he was born in Santa Maria. When he moved to Massachusetts, he brought with him twenty-seven slaves. He later sold his slave plantation in Santa Maria and donated the proceeds of the sale to start Harvard Law School.

Terrence wondered if Thoreau knew about Harvard Law School's connection to slavery. Thoreau attended Harvard and completed his studies there in 1837. He read Thoreau's writings hoping that he would see a reference to Santa Maria and its slave connection to Harvard Law School, but none was present.

Royalls was not the first sugar estate in Santa Maria. It was a prominent one but not the most significant. The first sugar estate in Santa Maria was Betty's Hope. It was named after the owner's daughter. It was the flagship estate in Santa Maria.

The history of Caribbean from the inception of African slavery, is a history of murder and exploitation of African people who were brought to the shores of the islands and made to work for three hundred and fifty years without remuneration. If the African slaves dared to show dissent for their exploitation, they faced certain death.

Terrence tried to imagine what life was like on a sugar plantation during the time of slavery. Yes, he had read about it and knew that slavery was officially abolished on August 1st 1834, but he knew that he could not really know the horrors of the time.

Though he did not officially live on an estate, he had connections with some. One in particular was Betty's Hope, the first sugar plantation in Santa Maria. His aunt, the one he lived with after his mother had died and his father terrorized him and his siblings upon his return to Santa Maria, had lived there with her family. Her husband was the manager of this sugar plantation in the 1950's before he lost his job and the family moved to the city. The irony of it was that this estate house, with its deep connections to slavery and exploitation, was now occupied by blacks who had become managers and overseers. Terrence's, great aunt, the one who raised his mother and his aunt, worked as a field hand on the estate while the niece that she raised lived in the main estate house as the wife of the manager of the estate.

Terrence's mother and her sister had been raised by an aunt because their mother had migrated to New York City in 1925 and left her two daughters ages seven and five with her sister with the intention of sending for them to join her as soon as she could afford to do so. She was twenty-seven years old when she arrived in New York City via Ellis Island.

Terrence had met his grandmother only once before he went to live in New York City. When he was a small boy, he had heard of his grandmother but only knew that she lived in a different country. He knew that from time to time, a barrel of second-hand clothes would arrive, and he was told that his grandmother had sent it. There was at least one item of clothing in the barrel for each member of the family and for each member of his aunt's family as well. She returned to Santa Maria for a visit when Terrence was about twelve years old. He remembered her as an older lady that everyone paid deference to. At the time of her visit, Terrence and his siblings had already moved from their father's house and were living with their aunt, his grandmother's other daughter. One day his grandmother told him that she was taking him to meet his grandfather whom he had never met and knew nothing about. It was a Thursday afternoon, he remembered it well because he and his grandmother were driven there by his eldest cousin who was off work that afternoon. In Santa Maria, retail stores were closed on Thursdays and his cousin was off from work that afternoon.

At the time, it did not occur to him that he was the only one of the children who was being taken by his grandmother to meet their grandfather. Terrence remembers arriving at an estate house in the north of the island and his grandmother getting out of the car and telling Terrence and his cousin to wait for her. They both waited silently in the car for her to return. Twenty minutes passed and she returned and told Terrence to come with her. In the front of the house was a big gallery and there were a number of steps leading up to this gallery. The steps were quite high and lead to a gate in the center of the gallery. They got to the top of the steps, entered the gate, crossed the gallery and entered a large living room. There was a lady in the room and someone lying on a bed in the corner. His grandmother walked him over to the man lying in the bed in the corner of the living room and said,

"This is your grandfather."

She looked down at the man and said,

"This is your grandson."

When Terrence looked at the man, he noticed two things immediately. The first thing he noticed was that the man lying on the bed in corner of the room that his grandmother said was his grandfather was a white man. The second thing that he noticed was that the man did not open his eyes. He was blind. Terrence stood and looked at the man and did not say anything. He felt uncomfortable and awkward just standing there. He stood there for about a minute and his grandmother perhaps saw his discomfort and told him that he could go back to the car. Once back in the car, he sat and waited with his cousin for their grandmother to return. It would be the first and only time that he would ever see his grandfather. In the coming years, he walked by the house many times because it was on the way to his favorite beach, the one he frequented most often with his friends when he became a teenager and was allowed to go to the beach without being accompanied by a family member. He never told his friends that his grandfather lived in the house that they walked by almost every Saturday or Sunday on their way to the beach.

The day after his grandmother took him to the house of his grandfather, she returned to New York City. He would not see her again until he moved there in June of 1970. When he went back home with his grandmother after he saw the blind white man that she said was his grandfather, he wanted to ask her many questions but did not. He thought of him only as a blind, old white man. He had questions that he wanted to ask. Who is he? Why haven't I met him before? Did my mother know him? Why didn't he attend my mother's funeral? How did you know him? What kind of work did he do? He later found the answers on his own.

There were so many questions he wanted to ask but he did not. He did not know if his grandmother was willing or even able to answer the questions which he had. He did not know her well, so he refrained from asking.

Terrence later learned that his mother's father became blind late in his life because he suffered from glaucoma. He also learned that his mother's father, a white man, had several children with black women. He also learned that he did not publicly acknowledge any of his children with black women and also did not support any of them financially or otherwise. He learned that his mother's father did not attend his mother's funeral because he did not think of her as his daughter. He knew that it was his daughter, but he felt no obligation or responsibility to take care of any of his children with black women. He also learned that he had an uncle, his mother's brother, who was fathered by this man lying on the bed in the living room who had been blinded by glaucoma. He learned that his uncle suffered the indignity of being rejected by his mother's husband because he served as a reminder that his wife had sex with a white man, even though it occurred before they met, and bore him a son. It is not known if the sex was consensual, she was an employee in their kitchen. Because of this, Terrence's uncle, after being rejected by his mother's husband and by extension his mother, had to live with his grandmother before he was sent off to live and fend for himself in England as a teenager and never returned to Santa Maria.

Terrence learned that his mother's father had been an estate manager from a family which had moved to Santa Maria from

England in the nineteenth century. Several sons were in the family and the sons were not reluctant to father children that they did not support.

Terrence's mother had not been acknowledged by her white father at her birth in May of 1920. His name does not appear on her birth certificate, thus in his eyes, relinquishing of any responsibility of fatherhood. This practice was directly passed on from slavery when the slave owners and estate managers fathered many children with slaves and went on to keep their offspring in slavery. He spent his last years before his death in blindness. Terrence wondered if this was karma for the harm he had caused his mother and the other children that he had with black women. At five years old, Terrence's mother was left in the care of her aunt who raised her. Her mother had left for New York City, and never returned to live permanently in Santa Maria. At thirty-two, Terrence's mother had mothered six children and ventured to raise them on her own after the birth of her sixth child, Terrence. At thirty-nine, she died at the hands of a doctor who caused her to bleed to death from a botched, relatively minor surgery.

It was her mother's intention to have her join her in New York City at a later date but that never came to fruition. When Terrence's grandmother arrived in Harlem in 1925 without a formal education, she was twenty-seven years old and only had the experience of working on the sugar estate, Betty's Hope as a field hand. The same estate where her older daughter would later live and raise her children in the great house as the wife of the estate manager.

Upon her arrival in Harlem, she became a cleaning lady and did this job for many years up to the time she was of the age to receive her Social Security benefits. Terrence learned that his grandmother was a cleaning lady because he accompanied her to work one day. During the summer that he arrived he was spending time with her while she lived in the Bronx. She had moved from her small kitchenette in Harlem to a spacious apartment in the Bronx. The move became necessary because she needed more room when she had sent for two of Terrence's sisters to live with her. The first one arrived in 1963 and the second one arrived in 1964. She asked Terrence to accompany her to work and he did. It was if she wanted him to know what she did for a living. That morning she woke up early and got dressed. She wore a lovely dress and shoes which could have been worn to church. She also wore her ever present hat which was customary for ladies in Santa Maria when they were going out.

They walked to the subway station and took the train to Harlem. When they got to their destination, she rang the doorbell for one of the apartments in a five-story building. The door buzzed and his grandmother pushed the door and it opened and they entered the building. She knocked on the door of one of the apartments on the ground floor. A lady answered the door and they entered the apartment. Terrence was told to sit in the living room while his grandmother went into a back room. When she came out of the back room ten minutes later, she had changed her clothes. She was wearing clothes that she had put in a bag which she had brought with her. The clothes were not at all like the clothes she wore there. These clothes were old and worn and she was not wearing the hat, she had her head tied with a cloth which reminded him of the cloth that ladies working in the cane fields of Santa Maria would wear. She was also wearing old tennis shoes. They both left the apartment and went into the hallway. In the hallway, she opened the door of a storage closet and took out a bucket, a broom and a mop along with cleaning supplies. They then walked up the five flights of stairs to the top floor. When they got there, she filled the bucket from the faucet in the storage closet on that floor. She started by sweeping the entire common area of the floor which had four apartments. After sweeping the floor, she diligently mopped it.

This action on her part was continued from floor to floor. Each took about an hour to complete. She did her work diligently and when she completed each floor, it was spotless. After she completed the fifth and fourth floors she stopped and offered Terrence one of the two cheese sandwiches which she had made and packed in her bag before they left her home that morning. After eating her sandwich, she continued her work. When she completed all the floors, she packed the supplies back into the storage closet on the first floor and once again knocked on the door of the apartment on the first floor where she had changed her clothes. They went into the apartment where she changed back into the clothes she had worn from home. When they said their goodbyes to the lady who was in the apartment, he noticed that his grandmother had been given an envelope that he assumed was the pay for the work which she had done.

On the train ride back to the Bronx, his grandmother barely spoke and neither did Terrence. It was the first time that Terrence had become aware that his grandmother was a cleaning lady.

This was her job for the past forty-five years that she had been living in the United States. In those forty-five years, she had managed to help with the support of her two daughters who had been left behind when she migrated. She had also managed to help with the support of her second daughter's children after her death and after the abuse they had suffered from their father. This she had done on the salary of a cleaning lady.

The experience of seeing his grandmother clean the hallways of a five-story building on this day was an awakening for Terrence. It gave him a better understanding that sacrifices had to be made in order to accomplish your goals. He got the feeling that she wanted him to see what her work entailed. In her own way, he felt that she was telling him that despite what she did for a living, she still worked and lived with dignity. She was not defined by what she did for a living, she was defined by working hard and helping her family members who had not been able to live in the United States.

Terrence's two sisters arrived in New York city travelling on visitor's visas. They both managed, with the assistance of their grandmother, to obtain student visas which enabled them to remain longer in the United States. She did not send for her own daughters because her circumstances had been difficult, but she sent for her granddaughters and tried her best to ensure that they had a better life. She also tried her best to assist the other grand children in Santa Maria to ensure that they did not live in abject poverty.◊◊

Chapter 8

In his final year of college, Terrence was looking forward to his graduation. He had stopped driving the yellow cab and only worked part time at the bank. Instead of working more than forty hours per week he was working only twenty-five. He was on the Dean's List during his junior year, and it was his goal to be on the Dean's List during his final year. The reduced workload, he thought, would enable him to maximize his study time and it would allow him to achieve this academic accolade again. As he got closer and closer to becoming a college graduate, he thought about his first experience applying for a job with the Action Airline Agency and how he was refused without even given a chance to prove himself. He always remembered how the receptionist had strongly recommended that he should take a position as a messenger because he was not born in the United States. It was an indignity he did not want to experience after he graduated from college.

During this year, more students from the Caribbean entered St. Francis. The students were mostly from the larger islands such as Trinidad and Jamaica. There were a few from the smaller islands like Barbados, even though most people from Barbados did not consider their island to be small, it was only 166 square miles. A few like Terrence and his friend, Ira, were from the tiny islands of Santa Maria and St. Kitts. In his senior year, two students from Guyana arrived at St. Francis. Guyana was previously known as British Guiana before it became an independent country. Guyana is not an island in the Caribbean. Guyana is located in northern South America next to Venezuela, Suriname and Brazil. Guyana is a huge country compared to the islands of the Caribbean. Guyanese as the people from this country are called, often point out to people from the small islands that they are South Americans. The first meeting of a person from Guyana and a person from another island might go like this:

Person from the Caribbean saying to the Guyanese,

"Where are you from?"

Guyanese response,

"I am from South America."

Caribbean person,

"Really, South America, where in South America?"

Guyanese response,

"Guyana."

Caribbean person looking disappointed,

"You are from Guyana, why didn't you just say that the first time?"

Caribbean people have considered Guyana to be a part of the Caribbean. This is partly due to the fact that it is the only country in South America that speaks English as its first language, and it is also the only country in South America whose cricketers are eligible to play for the West Indies cricket team. It was easier to just say Guyana, but it was more interesting to say South America. Saying South America added an air of mystery and magic. It also gave them an opportunity to project themselves as superior to others from the islands of the

Caribbean, even though Guyana was one of the poorest countries in the region.

Two girls from Guyana enrolled at St. Francis during the start of Terrence's senior year. During introductions, they said that they were from South America, but it was quickly deduced that they were, in fact, from Guyana, which they confirmed when asked. These girls did not appear to be poor and gave no indication that they were. To the contrary, they gave the impression that they were from well to do families. They said that they were first cousins. These two cousins did not appear to be academically inclined instead they seemed to be more interested in the social aspects of university life. Unlike other first year students, they socialized with seniors and were quite comfortable doing so. They were not like the other girls from the Caribbean islands who were more reserved. They did not adhere to the protocols that were observed in a normal college setting relative to status and seniority. In the cafeteria, the Caribbean students commanded an area of ten tables. Various groups and fraternities within the college commanded their own areas. Within those areas which were unofficially established for certain groups, there were further areas of specificity relative to seating arrangement based on your seniority on campus. There were tables for freshmen, sophomores, juniors and seniors. It was unusual for freshmen to sit at a table that was generally used by seniors unless they were invited to do so. These two girls from Guyana did not sit at the freshmen tables but they generally sat at the senior tables with male seniors. The male seniors did not object because these two girls, who said that they were cousins, were extremely attractive and outgoing.

In conversations, they referred to the Prime Minister of Guyana as their uncle. Terrence was taken aback by this, but he was also intrigued by their conversations. They gave the impression that they were from prominent families in Guyana and that they were only in the United States for a short period of time and upon the completion of their degree, they would return to Guyana to fit right back into the upper classes of Guyanese society to which they belonged and in which they felt most comfortable. They were oblivious to the fact that they made other students uncomfortable with some of the things which they said. They did not fail to tell their fellow students that they had maids and drivers who chauffeured them to the places that they wanted to go.

They gave the impression that attending college was simply an inconvenience that they had to endure for four years. A college degree was not required or necessary for them to lift themselves out of poverty and to help their families. Getting a college degree was only a formality, their place in Guyanese society had already been established by virtue of their parents' positions. One day, one of them was asked if it was her mother or father who was a sibling of the Prime Minister. The student who asked this question made the assumption after hearing her refer to the Prime Minister as her uncle. She explained that he was not actually her uncle but because her father and the Prime Minister were friends, then it was the polite thing to do to refer to him as uncle. It was a sign of respect. She did not necessarily appear to be bragging when she spoke about their life in Guyana. It seemed normal to her. She did not seem to conceptualize that some of the other students from the Caribbean who attended St. Francis were from backgrounds which were completely different to hers.

One day, Terrence was sitting at a table in the cafeteria having lunch and she casually told a story of her thrill at being picked up at her home by her uncle's driver in her uncle's new Bentley. She described the Bentley in detail and said that she was picked up and taken to the Prime Minister's home because she had an appointment with his daughter to go swimming in their large pool.

While she spoke, she had a disconcerting habit of having a straight pin in the corner of her month. Terrence told her that it was not only odd for her to have a straight pin in her mouth, but it was also dangerous because it could be swallowed. When she was told that it was dangerous and could be swallowed, she said that she had swallowed straight pins on two separate occasions and had to be taken to the hospital where her stomach was x-rayed to verify that the pins indeed had been swallowed. On both occasions, she had to remain in the hospital and monitored until the doctors were assured that the pins had left her body. She insisted that she was attempting to stop this bizarre habit, but it was difficult.

At the time, the Guyanese scholar and intellectual, Dr. Walter Rodney had returned to Guyana after teaching at the University of the West Indies in Jamaica and the University of Dar es Salaam in Tanzania. He had entered politics and was an opponent of the establishment and consequently was an opponent of the Prime Minister who, it was said, held on to power by creating divisions in the various ethnic groups that made up the Guyanese population. Still in his twenties, Dr. Walter Rodney was widely respected and recognized as scholar. The power structures in the Caribbean were afraid of his message of unifying the people from all various backgrounds regardless of differences real or imagined. At twenty-four, he obtained a doctorate in African History and had written a book entitled, *How Europe Underdeveloped Africa*. The book was widely read in academic circles and brought him respect and recognition around the world.

During a conversation, she was asked what she thought of Dr. Walter Rodney and her response was brief. She simply said with sincerity,

"He is a troublemaker."

She offered no further explanation when asked to do so. Terrence got the feeling that she was repeating what she had heard. Her 'uncle,' the Prime Minister, thought that Dr. Walter Rodney was a troublemaker and that was the narrative that permeated the political discourse from the Prime Minister and his party.

Terrence felt sorry for these two girls from Guyana. They were in the United States studying with the intention of obtaining a college degree and returning home to rejoin the upper class of their society. They would, in all probability, be able to get good jobs in the government using their political connections. He felt sad for not only for these two young women, but he also felt sad for the people of the Guyana whose politicians used division as a means to obtain and keep power.

Unlike most girls from other Caribbean islands, these two cousins from Guyana were smokers. In Caribbean society, it was not only unusual for girls to smoke cigarettes, but it was also frowned upon. One day, while having lunch, one of them was asked why she smoked, and her response was quite casual.

"I have been smoking for a long time. When I was twelve, my sister and I would steal my father's cigarettes and smoke them upstairs in my bedroom. It was so much fun. One time, my room caught on fire by accident because a match fell to the floor and the rug was on fire and our house almost burned down because the fire spread quickly. Our father was upset and told us not to take his cigarettes anymore. He had to get workers from the Department of Housing and Planning to come over to fix the house. So the house was fixed rather quickly. I should have listened to him and stopped taking his cigarettes, but I did not and now I smoke a pack a day, but I am trying to reduce it and eventually stop."

At the end of the first semester that they attended St. Francis, the two cousins announced that they were transferring to another college. They did not return for the second semester and no one heard from them again.

Besides these two cousins, Terrence had known only one other person from Guyana. Danny was a young man in his mid-twenties when they met. They met shortly after Terrence's father had died and they had sold the cleaners to a friend of their father. Danny lived on Madison Avenue in the building next to where Terrence lived. Danny was murdered at 7:10pm on a Saturday night by the superintendent of his building who was an old, deranged man. The circumstances of his murder affected Terrence for a very long time. The murder was senseless.

On Saturday nights, when Terrence was at home, he would go downstairs at about 6:30pm and chat with Danny and the new owner of the cleaners. The owner wanted Danny and Terrence to be there for his closing time which was at 7:00pm. He felt that it was unlikely that he would be robbed if he had company during closing time. On this particular Saturday night, Terrence was in the cleaners with Danny at 6:00pm and anticipated staying there until closing time at 7:00pm. At about 6:15pm, he was suffering from a headache and decided to go upstairs to his apartment to take medicine and to lie down for a while with the hope that his headache would have subsided before 7:00pm and then return to the cleaners. His headache did not subside, and he decided to stay in bed. At 7:15pm he heard the sounds of emergency vehicles outside. He looked out of his bedroom window and saw an ambulance and fire truck outside of the building where Danny lived. He thought nothing of it and returned to bed. It was not unusual to see emergency vehicles in Harlem. The following day was Sunday, Terrence went downstairs and saw Danny's next-door neighbor sitting on the steps of their building. The neighbor had his head bowed. Terrence walked over, said hello and asked if Danny was inside. The neighbor barely looked up and said,

"Danny is dead."

Terrence could not believe what he was hearing and said,

"What?"

The neighbor repeated what he had said and added,

"Danny is dead, the super killed him last night when he was entering his apartment."

The neighbor went on to say that when Danny was opening the door of his apartment with his key, the super came up behind him with a meat cleaver and literally split his head open, killing him almost instantly.

Terrence knew that Danny had had a disagreement with the super regarding properly heating the building. It was November and it was getting quite cold and Danny, who had a wife and a young baby, asked the super to put the heat on because it was cold in the mornings and in the nights. The super who was not a stable man, took offense at Danny's insistence that he put the heat on, retaliated by murdering him with a meat cleaver. It was a tragic circumstance beyond reason.

After murdering Danny, the super took off and could not be located for over a week. When he was captured by the police, they found him to be incoherent and suffering from dementia. He was put on trial for the murder but was given a minimal prison sentence of two years because of his mental state.

Terrence agonized about the murder of his friend because it was so senseless. He regretted that he had not gone back down to the cleaners at closing time. He often chatted with Danny after they witnessed the closing of the cleaners. He thought that maybe if he had gone back down to the cleaners, Danny would not have gone home immediately, and he would not have come in contact with the super. It took him a while to come to grips with the reality that it was not his fault; he could have done nothing to change what happened that fateful Saturday night where Danny's wife lost her husband and Danny's baby lost her father for no apparent reason other than the psychosis which haunted this old man. It seemed so unfair. Danny was just a young man who had migrated to the United States in search of a better life, and he was making gains towards that outcome. Danny too had been a tailor and was working in the garment district. He was not making a lot of money, but he was making enough to make ends meet. He just wanted his apartment to be warm for the comfort of his wife and daughter and he lost his life for making this simple request to the person who was responsible for ensuring that the tenants were comfortable.

Terrence's graduation was now not far off and he and his family were now living in the East Flatbush area of Brooklyn after moving from Harlem. The family move was necessitated by a robbery and a shooting. The shooting took place in the hallway of the first floor as you entered the building on Madison Avenue.

Mr. Benson lived on the fourth floor across the hall from Terrence and his siblings. Mr. Benson was the owner of the candy store on the ground floor of the building. One entrance to the store was located on Madison Avenue and the other entrance was on 125th Street. The candy store was popular with the neighborhood kids who shopped there for sweets and sodas. The candy store was also popular with adults from the neighborhood who played the numbers. Playing the numbers was a big part of life in Harlem at the time. Invariably, as in other enterprises that were illegal, there is always trouble lurking around the corner. This trouble comes about because of jealousy, or some perceived wrong-doing or from the competitors. Mr. Benson, from all appearances, was a kind man who lived what appeared to be a normal life as a small business owner.

On a normal Friday morning as Mr. Benson entered the building, he saw two men who had been hiding under the staircase, emerge with guns in their hands. Mr. Benson had already entered the hallway and closed the door. He attempted to exit the hallway using the door that he had just closed but he was unable to do so. He was shot several times in the back and left to die on the floor.

Terrence was at school that morning of the shooting, but he saw the blood on the floor and the walls of the hallway when he arrived home. He was told of the shooting before he entered the hallway to go upstairs to their apartment. He was told by the new owner of the cleaners. The owner was a friend of Terrence's father to whom the cleaners was sold after his father had died and the decision was made to sell it because none of the siblings wanted to keep and maintain it.

Terrence had heard about the 'numbers' but had never played it. All he knew about the 'numbers' was that it was spoken about by almost all of the residents of Harlem. Participants chose a number and told that number to a 'number runner' who came around each day. Usually, the number runner would write the number down on a piece of paper. The number runner would then be given a sum of money to put on the number that was told to him and which he wrote on a piece of paper. There are stories about number runners who could memorize the numbers of all their customers and the sums of money which had been placed on each number chosen. This was done so that if a number runner was apprehended by the police, he did not have the numbers chosen on his person but in his head. He could not be prosecuted because he had no evidence on him.

Being a number runner could be quite dangerous at times, this was particularly so if the number runner was dishonest. His dishonesty could lead to him being seriously hurt or even the loss of his life. Dishonest number runners would take money from customers and did not turn the money in to be recorded by the higher ups in the number running organization. If a person placed ten dollars on a particular number that day and the number became the winning number, then the customer would be expected to receive his payoff amounting to several thousand dollars. If the number runner had been dishonest and did not submit the number to be recorded, then the number runner would be in deep trouble because he did not have the money to pay the winner. This became more ominous if there were several winners on a particular day.

Number runners were a part of a criminal organization and the higher ups in the organization did not like when their runners did not submit the money to be recorded. This meant the number runners, if they didn't submit the money, were stealing not only from the customers but also from the organization. Mr. Benson was not a low-level number runner, he was more of a middleman, so Terrence believed that he was not killed for stealing, he figured it must have been some other reason maybe he had become too much of a strong competitor and the decision was made to kill him. After his death, there were rumors that he was also involved with the selling of heroin. Heroin addiction was a major scourge on life in Harlem at the time. Terrence had learned that you did not have to know what your neighbors did for a living. He learned his lesson from the 'blind' man whom he had seen on the train. Terrence had learned that it was best to just mind his own 'fucking' business as the blind man advised. Mr. Benson lived directly across the hall and the only thing that Terrence knew about him was that he owned the candy store on the corner. He was oblivious to his other activities which became known only after his death.

The experience of having to enter the hallway and see all the blood of his neighbor who had been killed that very morning, gave him an uneasy feeling and he thought maybe it was time for them to move. The siblings discussed the matter, and the decision was indeed made for them to move but because of lack of funds and the deposit needed on a new apartment, they decided that the move would not be made immediately but in six months.

Before those six months were up their apartment was robbed. Terrence came home from school and found three persons in their apartment. Usually, he went to his job at the bank directly after school but on this day, he did not feel well and called in sick. Upon arriving at their apartment, he unlocked the door. To his surprise, he heard the door lock again from the inside. He also heard footsteps and voices coming from inside the apartment. He knew that no one was supposed to be at home and the danger that he sensed was palpable. He immediately ran down the stairs and used the phone in the cleaners to call the police. After calling the police, two men who were in their late teens or early twenties ran out of the building and headed north on Madison Avenue, he tried to follow them from a comfortable distance, but they turned left on 126th Street and ran even faster. Terrence turned around and stood outside of his building. As he stood there, a young woman came out of the building with a shopping cart stuffed with items taken from their apartment. The most prominent item that was protruding from the top of the cart was his sister's small black and white television set. He did not confront the young woman who appeared to be a heroin addict. It was not necessary for him to confront her because the police were arriving and as they got out of their squad car, he approached them and told them that she was one of the persons who had broken into their apartment. She had made no attempt to run or to escape. She seemed to be to so high on heroin that she would have been unable to run even if she had tried. She was arrested on the spot and Terrence was told that he had to accompany them to the police station if he wanted to file a complaint.

The shopping cart with the stolen items were placed in the trunk of the police car and Terrence sat in the back of the car with the heroin addicted thief who had broken into their apartment. The difference was that she was in handcuffs and he was not. The two officers sat in the front of the car. The police station was only four blocks away on Lexington Avenue and 123rd Street. When they got to the police station, the officers took her into a back room where she was processed and arrested. When the officers returned to take a statement from Terrence, they unpacked the shopping car and placed the items on the counter. One of the items placed on the counter was a toaster. The toaster somehow fell to the ground and out of it came at least twenty small roaches which scurried around the floor to find safety. One police officer, upon seeing the scurrying roaches yelled, 'holy shit' and the two of them smashed them with their shoes. Terrence stood there watching the officers kill the roaches that had come out of the toaster and hoped that a hole would open in the floor of the police station through which he could fall.

After killing the roaches, the officers turned to Terrence and took his statement. He tried not to show his embarrassment, but it was evident. He was told that the lady would probably be released the next day and that she would be given a date to appear in court but that it was unlikely that she would turn up for her court date. He was also told that he would be notified at a later time of the court date and he could appear to testify against her if she did in fact appear. Terrence received the court date in the mail and showed up to the courthouse on time but was told by the officers that the drug addicted lady who had broken into their apartment and had been caught with stolen items, including the toaster with roaches, did not appear in court. He was told that he could take back the items including the toaster, which had been kept as evidence. He told the personnel at the court that he did not want them and asked for them to be thrown away.

After this break-in, Terrence and his siblings moved to East Flatbush, an area in Brooklyn that until recently, had been predominantly a Jewish community. The Jewish families were moving out to other areas of Brooklyn and Queens and families from the Caribbean were moving in.

At the end of the first semester of his senior year, Terrence had completed the majority of his coursework in English and education that would enable him to obtain a degree in English and Teaching Training. The Teaching Training part of his degree would allow him to become a teacher. The major undertaking he was required to complete was student teaching. All candidates who wished to qualify as teachers were required to complete a course as a student teacher. Terrence was assigned to an Intermediate School 293 in Red Hook, Brooklyn. Red Hook was considered to be a poor neighborhood and many of the students were from Puerto Rico and Central America. Within the middle school, Terrence was assigned to a male English teacher named Mr. Eiser. Terrence was supposed to learn the fundamentals and nuances of teaching from Mr. Eiser. Terrence observed Mr. Eiser closely and came to the conclusion that he was not a very caring teacher. He carried out the functions of his job but did nothing to motivate or encourage his students to excel. Terrence had overheard him refer to his students, while speaking to another teacher, as 'immigrants' who barely spoke English.

Student teachers were required to take over one of the periods after two weeks as student teacher, but Mr. Eiser did not allow Terrence to take over the class. Terrence reported the matter to the director of Student Teaching at St. Francis who then conferred with the principal of the school. Mr. Eiser was told to allow Terrence to take over one of the periods. He was not happy with the directions given by the principal.

After this circumstance, the relationship with Terrence and Mr. Eiser became less cordial but more perfunctory in nature. Terrence tried his best to communicate with the students and to encourage them as much as possible. He encouraged them to come to see him after school for extra help if they needed it. Mr. Eiser did not help students after class and encouraged Terrence not to do this because in his words, 'the students were lazy, and this practice supported their laziness.'

Just as Terrence decided at an early age that he would not become a man like his father, before he completed his student teaching, he decided he would not be a teacher like Mr. Eiser. At the end of his student teaching, the 'lazy' students had bought him a present and a card. The students wished him good luck and thanked him for helping them after school. He also thanked them for their kindness and thoughtfulness. He wished them well and encouraged them to do their best. He told them all that they could be successful, but they had to do their best and to put forward a serious effort to accomplish their goals. He asked them if they wanted to make their parents proud. They said that they did, and he encouraged them to do so by taking advantage of the opportunities which their parents never had. He understood clearly that students did not care how much a teacher knew about the subject matter being taught and what they could learn from the teacher unless the teacher was able to communicate that he cared about them. Caring was essential to the learning process.

With the completion of his student teaching, Terrence knew that he had made the right decision in becoming a teacher. He felt that he could make a difference especially to students who needed a chance. He felt that an education was the great equalizer, no matter the circumstances of a person's birth and circumstances of a person's life, success was attainable with effort and hard work. He knew that an education, once attained, could never be taken away from an individual.

As a teacher, he relished the challenge that he was undertaking to make a difference in the lives of his students.

On June 18, 1975, five years to the day that he arrived in New York City and had been put out of the taxi on the sidewalk at 125th Street and Madison Avenue by a fearful cab driver, Terrence walked across the stage of the Brooklyn Academy of Music, the venue for the St. Francis College graduating ceremony, and received a college degree in English and Teacher Training. He had become the first member of his family and extended family to receive a college degree. In the audience to witness his graduation were his siblings and his grandmother, the grandmother whom everyone referred to as Aunt Kitty, who had worked as a field hand at the former slave plantation and one of the oldest in the Caribbean, Betty's Hope Estate. The grandmother who had left her two daughters, Bernice and Ruby, in the care of her sister to seek a better life in the United States with the hope of having them join her at a later date but was unable to do so because of her limited education. Her daughter, Bernice had allowed the six children of her sister, Ruby to live with her and her family because she had a dream. In the dream her sister, Ruby, had asked her not to allow her children to return to their father's house.

Aunt Kitty, his grandmother, exuded quiet pride in the college graduation of her grandson on whose shoulders family expectations now rested.

◊◊

Epilogue

In 1949 Terrence's father moved his wife and the four children that he had with her to the southern Caribbean island of Curacao to work at the Shell Oil Refinery located there. Before uprooting his family to go to Curacao, he had been a tailor in Pares Village, where he met Terrence's mother. She was born in the village to Catherine Thomas and Fred Abbott who were not married and in all probability were not in love. Catherine Thomas was black, and Fred Abbott was white. They were from different worlds, but it was not unusual for white men of means to take sexual advantage of poor black women. At the time, she worked as a field hand on Betty's Hope Estate on the eastern side of the island and he was being groomed by his father to become an estate manager. Fred Abbott did not acknowledge the daughter he had with Catherine Thomas. His name does not appear on her birth certificate. Her birth certificate does not show a last name. It is an indignity that is bestowed on black children whose parents were not married. This practice is a remnant of slavery. It was a law instituted by the British in the Caribbean which they thought absolved the British men of raping their black slaves and sometimes having children with the women that they raped.

It was not known if the birth of Terrence's mother was the result of her being raped. What was known was that Fred Abbott was accused of rape by a black lady in Parham who bore him a daughter. The lady said that she was on her way home and was walking through a cane field when he came upon her riding his horse as the estate overseers and managers usually did. She had in her hand a stalk of sugar cane and he accused her of stealing it. He gave her a quid pro quo. Have sex with him or he would call the police and make a report that she was a thief who had illegally gone into the field and stole the stalk of sugar cane. She was totally afraid and traumatized at the prospect of being arrested. He recognized her fear and proceeded to dismount his horse. She did not resist. When he was finished, he mounted his horse and rode away. Nine months afterwards she gave birth to a daughter whose birth certificate does not bear his name. That child was the sister of Terrence's mother, who might have also come into the world in the same manner. It would have been bad if this was the only known case of this type of abuse of power and sexual perversion but there were others.

Terrence's childhood friend, one of the boys, with whom he made the fateful trip to see Luz Fernandez at the Daitch Shopwell on 125th Street, had a great uncle who was born in similar circumstances. His grandmother's sister was walking home after a long day working on a sugar estate. On her way, she saw a mango tree and stopped to pick a ripe mango. As she was picking the mango, an overseer came riding up on his horse. She too was given the same quid pro quo, have sex with the overseer or be arrested for stealing a mango. Out of this circumstance a male child was born to a scared sixteen-year-old. The name of the father did not appear on the birth certificate of the great uncle of Terrence's friend.

These father rapists felt that because their names did not appear on the birth certificates of their offspring, they were absolved of all responsibility. This might have been so from a legal perspective, but it could not absolve them of the hate bestowed upon them by their victims or the hate of their children when they found out the circumstance under which they were conceived. The overseers and estate managers who carried out these cases of overt rape and sexual abuse were from prominent white families and were landowners. In most cases they ignored their black children and left them to suffer in poverty.

History has a way of judging wrongdoing. There is a general belief that children should not be held accountable for the wrongdoing of their parents. On the surface, that seems pretty straight forward if there is a belief in the concept of personal responsibility for one's actions. The situation becomes less straight forward when the question becomes whether or not a person should be able to benefit from the wrongdoing of his parents. The white offspring of these father rapists in most cases, inherited vast wealth from them. These father rapists always married women from other white families and continued to grow their wealth. Their white offspring in most cases benefitted handsomely from the wrongdoing by virtue of the fact that a part of their wealth inherited from their parent was accumulated by not spending a penny to raise or care for the children they had fathered with black women. There is no doubt that their white offspring benefitted from the callous actions of their father rapists.

Terrence's father had heard that workers were needed in the oil refinery in Curacao. He had travelled out of Santa Maria only once before. He had gone to Cuba when he was thirty-six to find his mother who had abandoned him when he was a baby. She had placed her two sons in the care of her mother who lived in the village of Freetown and migrated to Cuba. Many persons from the other islands of the Caribbean had migrated to Cuba to work in the sugar cane fields of the island. He found his mother living in Mayaguez with her new family. She was married and had two children with her husband. He was happy to meet the woman whom he had last seen when he was four years old, but she did not appear to be happy to see him. He got the feeling that he had interrupted her life. He felt a sense of rejection. He returned to Santa Maria and made no effort to contact his mother again. He felt the pain of being rejected by his mother as a child and as a man.

Curacao did not have any natural deposits of oil, but it had one of the largest oil refineries in the world. Shell Oil Company had built this large oil refinery in an area of the capital called

Punda. In the early 1940's, oil was discovered in Lake Maracaibo in Venezuela. It was determined that this lake had one of the largest deposits of oil in the world. Shell Oil was one of the companies that was contracted to help the Venezuelan government to process and refine the oil. Shell Oil determined that Venezuela was not stable and wanted to protect their investment. They opted to build the oil refinery in Curacao which had a stable government and was still a colony of Holland. Curacao is located just off the coast of Venezuela and it was not difficult to drill the crude oil from Lake Maracaibo and then send it to Curacao to be refined. This circumstance caused the migration of many persons from the Eastern Caribbean to Curacao.

A similar situation occurred when the Panama Canal was built in the late 1800's. The Panama Canal took ten years to build and many persons from the Caribbean migrated to Panama to work. Another large migration took place in the 1920's as the Dominican Republic recruited persons to come there to cut sugar cane.

In November of 1950, a fifth child, a girl, was born into the Antonio family. Nineteen months later in 1952, the sixth and last child, Terrence, was born into the family on the island of Curacao. At the end of the year, Terrence's mother and her six children returned to Santa Maria to live permanently. Terrence was four months old.

Terrence and his sister who was also born in Curacao were never citizens of the country in which they were born. Santa Maria has a law which stipulates that any person born in Santa Maria is automatically a citizen of Santa Maria at birth. The law also stipulates that at birth you are automatically a citizen of Santa Maria if either one or both of your parents are citizens of Santa Maria. The law goes further to stipulate that you are a citizen of Santa Maria if either one or both of your grandparents are citizens of Santa Maria, regardless of the country where you are born.

The Constitution of the United States of America also stipulates that all persons born in the United States are citizens of the United States regardless of the status of the parents. On the other hand, many countries of the world stipulate that the granting of citizenship by being born in a country is not automatic. In many cases if you are born in a specific country to parents who are citizens of another country, you are not automatically granted citizenship. In the United Kingdom, you are not automatically granted citizenship if both of your parents are not citizens. In the State of Kuwait in the Middle East, it is very close to impossible to become a citizen if you are male and your parents, at the time of your birth, were not citizens. It is possible to be born in Kuwait and live there for your entire life and still have no avenue available for you to become a citizen if at the time of your birth your parents were not Kuwaiti.

Though Terrence and his sister above him were born on the island of Curacao, they were not citizens of Curacao. At birth, they were citizens of Santa Maria by virtue of the fact that both of their parents were born in Santa Maria and were citizens of Santa Maria. It is not known if they had remained in Curacao at what point they would have become citizens of that country, if at all. The question became moot because at the end of 1952, Terrence's mother took her six children back to Santa Maria. Her husband stayed behind and continued working for the Shell Oil Refinery.

◊◊

ABOUT THE AUTHOR

Ronan Matthew moved to New York and attended St. Francis College at the age of seventeen. He subsequently moved to Las Vegas where he attended Graduate School, earning a Doctoral degree in Educational Leadership, and worked in the Clark County school system for thirty years. He currently spends time between Las Vegas and his homeland, Antigua.

.

Printed in Great Britain
by Amazon

80517616R00119